T0196549

Until It's All Over

TERRY L. KEMP

authorHOUSE®

AuthorHouse™
1663 Liberty Drive
Bloomington, IN 47403
www.authorhouse.com
Phone: 1 (800) 839-8640

Published by AuthorHouse 04/05/2016

ISBN: 978-1-5246-0037-2 (sc)
ISBN: 978-1-5246-0028-0 (hc)
ISBN: 978-1-5246-0036-5 (e)

Library of Congress Control Number: 2016905043

Print information available on the last page.

For C, Ashie and Hazers, with all my love.

<u>Beginning</u>

Have you ever wondered what you will do the second you realize you have died? I mean really contemplated it? Have you ever thought you may have a few choices left? In life, no two people will make the exact same series of decisions. And in death, no one ever makes the same decisions either. Keep this in mind as you continue reading; choices are yours to make in life and after. However, as always, there will be consequences. My name is Zach Dawson. Come; let me tell you about choices. I know all about them now. I know more now than I ever could have imagined. One day I may even clean up the results of one of your choices. Me, or someone like me.

"Does he know yet?"
"No. It will be evident to him soon."

The day my life changed was not unexpected to me. It was the level and type of change that I was not prepared for. Until this day, I had always been career focused. I was constantly attempting to improve my standing within the large corporation I worked for. The best way I knew to do this was to simply outwork those around me. This work ethic did not involve stepping on people to climb the ladder. Rather, I simple beat everyone to the next rung.

"Meat Eater", that is how many of my superiors would describe me. Maximum effort was the only level I knew and this rapidly propelled me from one promotion to another. When it came to useful minutes in the day, I consumed as many as possible, and this got me noticed at every level I achieved. And in the world of home improvement companies, this was the only way to survive.

Best Building Supply had been in business for nearly two decades when I was lucky enough to get a job with them. Their growth exploded through the building boom which enveloped the southeastern US in the early 80's. As cities such as Atlanta and Charlotte and Orlando saw their populations and infrastructures grow, Best swooped in and opened store after store to capitalize.

I had begun my career with them by working in one of their stores just outside of Atlanta. In a corporation built on benefiting from opportunity the best way to rapidly climb was to emulate the efforts of the parent company.

So that's what I did, from the very first day to the very last. Fifteen years after that first hard, dirty day, I had ascended to the position of regional manager, working out of a satellite corporate office.

I knew Best was going to do some job cuts on that fateful day. We had all known for quite a while. The economic conditions had turned decidedly sour over the last twelve months and rumors were flying around about layoffs and downsizing. One analyst even went so far as to describe the coming conditions as "the perfect economic shit-storm." That type of description from numbers-oriented, fact-based and highly intelligent people was quite scary.

So, I was somewhat prepared. Prepared to the point of telling people I didn't think the layoffs would come from within our department. We had dwindled from a team of thirty-six just three years prior to only thirteen on this day. So, how could they cut us any more?

Well, they did cut that day and I was one of four let go. Throughout the morning I slowly packed up my things from the office into plain brown corporate packing boxes. In my mind, I actually thought if I moved slowly enough, someone with a high company standing would realize the error and reverse all of this madness. That person never came to see me.

Occasionally, colleagues would drop by as they heard the news. From their mouths would come condolences, but their eyes would scream thank God it wasn't me. It was somewhat empowering to know that I had gone through this terrible

4

process to this point and not actually died. I felt stronger than the terrified who came to say goodbye to me.

By lunchtime, I was sitting in my car in the parking deck, sad from the events of the day, but strangely excited about the future. Outside my car, I noticed a cardinal hopping from one empty parking space to another. He could care less about my current predicament. He just wanted to find his next meal. It was time to call Abby, my wife. My adrenaline was rising as I called from my cell.

"Hey baby." I said, trying to sound calm.

"Hey, how's it going?" Abby replied.

"Well, it………uh…it was pretty bad," I revealed, using pauses to suppress the welling emotions.

"Yeah, are you okay?" she asked.

"No, not really," I stammered. "They got me."

I told her the remainder of the story as I battled back my emotions. There was no stopping the tears at that point; they were going to come out now and they did. I explained to Abby how the company had cut almost one thousand positions and mine was unfortunately one of them. She cried as well. Neither of us had been through this type of event before. It was traumatic, numbing and intensely personal all at the same time. Thus began the changes that would affect everyone in our family.

That night, we explained to our children how sometimes, companies have to cut people's jobs in order to keep the company from losing too much money. The explanation, even from us, didn't help their lack of understanding.

"But why you?" was asked over and over by our nine and thirteen year old daughters.

Daniela, or Dani as we called her, was a kind and giving child. Even though she was thirteen, she had not given in to the temptation to act like her peers. While others around her had taken to bullying, teasing or worse, she had remained above the fray. She always came to the defense of the weaker kids and had stood her ground a few times against the stronger. Her small stature made this feat even more laudable and she would twist her dark curly hair and lower her brown eyes in embarrassment whenever retelling the story.

Carrie was nine at the time and she was much less fazed. She was a handful of energy and many times it would manifest itself in trouble. Like her older sister, she too had curly hair. However, hers had turned an auburn red very early in life. When you coupled her hair color with her dark green eyes, it was the perfect disguise. The looks of an angel with the acts of a mischievous, albeit innocent, little devil.

As the days passed, Dani continued to struggle inwardly with the circumstances we faced. Carrie continued on as a nine year old should, unfazed by reality. Luckily, Abby continued to have some semblance of normalcy in her working life. This provided the one and only pillar of stability we had.

The confusion and fear of the companies' decision to tell me they didn't want me anymore soon melted from the mind of Carrie. However, those feelings, along with the others that come

6

with becoming a teen, lingered in Daniella's mind. They remained both in her and within the walls of our house and grew in scope. I was clueless to the notion that these emotions were a main ingredient for our coming changes and the associated challenges we would be faced with.

As the next few weeks went by, I ran the entire gambit of emotions. Shock, anger, relief, optimism, depression and acceptance all were experienced. Some days I went through them all more than once. Anger seemed to be the one emotion that lingered the most. Even though I rarely showed the anger outwardly, it was always there. There, invisible and unable to manifest outwardly, while glowing like a hot coal inwardly.

Weeks soon turned into months and I was constantly looking for a similar job. All the while, the anger continued to simmer and grow. Periodically, I would watch the evening news and fantasize about the top story of the day being that of my former corporate employer completely going belly up. I had no idea how deep emotions really worked in the environment around me and what they could do.

It was slow and silent, and not even really mine at first, the anger. It and fear took root in my oldest daughter much earlier than me. Dani was old enough to understand the enormity of our situation, especially as time ticked away and I still didn't have a job.

Even though my wife worked, her salary would not sustain our accustomed standard of living for long. It was more comfort money than anything else as I had been the primary income source for many years now. Ultimately, we would completely switch roles as the economy continued to tank and no one seemed to be hiring at all.

Outwardly, Abby and I continued to keep a veil between financial reality and our children. Even with the effort to whitewash our current predicament, a screaming storm of uncertainty and teen angst festered in Dani. At school, she would confide in certain, select teachers, but those instances were rare. Soon, the battle began to surface in the form of small rebellions in class or outbursts at home that would quickly explode into emotional maelstroms, raging until quieted only by parental intervention or sleep.

I didn't notice any of these behaviors or emotions at first. Neither did Abby. Mrs. Johnson didn't notice in math class, too busy playing solitaire on the computer. Coach Stevenson didn't put it together in P.E, he just thought she was becoming more competitive and aggressive. But someone somewhere did notice. They saw the opening and raced through the open door. Something terrible came in to our home.

I read somewhere once, or saw it on TV, that a poltergeist sometimes manifests during times of high emotional conflux, especially around teen aged girls. Knowing now what I do, I can say this is only partially true. There is no such thing as a poltergeist in the Webster's sense; a disembodied spirit or supernatural force credited with certain malicious or disturbing phenomena. Throughout history, poltergeist phenomena has often been linked with teenaged girls and the myriad of emotions surrounding them. There is no doubt that the emotions do play a huge part in these appearances, but not as a poltergeist, rather, as a ghost.

They feed on emotions, these dead people. Growing strong or weak based on the availability of these simple feelings that we take for granted. Think about your own emotional history. How many times have you felt drained after a strong exposure to your own happiness, sadness or anger? Sadness is especially powerful. We have all cried and afterwards are always exhausted, tired from the outpouring of our feelings. Where do you think these feelings go? After all, they are a form of energy. Sometimes, they are wasted or evaporate. They are just gone. But many times, after you release them they are gobbled up, straight out of the air, without you ever knowing. These feelings can sustain. Sustain a life long ago thought to have been extinguished. And you never even know. Let me tell you how I found out about all of this.

My personal awakening didn't happen slowly like you would think. No. This was a slap in the face. It was an undermining of my own perception of what reality was; a direct attack on my own Faith in God. And I thought that finding out how hydrogenated oil was manufactured was life altering. Looking back now I realize just how naïve I was.

"Dad can you come up here?" Dani called down from her upstairs bedroom.

"Yep." I replied in frustration not wanting to miss any of the baseball game I was watching.

"You are supposed to be asleep, Dani. Why are you still up?" I asked.

"I can't sleep," she wined. "Every time I get comfortable, it feels like something is pushing down on me."

"Are you worried about school tomorrow?" I asked.

"No, I mean something is really pushing down on me," she exclaimed.

"That is probably just stress," I argued.

And then it happened. Not subtly, not softly, but with force and malice. My head was suddenly forced down. My chin violently impacted my chest. The muscles in my neck caught fire with pain from the sudden push. In my mind I was thinking, "What the hell was that!?" Once my eyes regained focus I looked around the room to see who had done this. Dani had slid herself across her bed and had her back against the wall, trying in vain to protect herself from whoever had done this to me. At least that is what I thought; who? But not in the sense that you are thinking of. No, I really expected to see someone else standing there in the room with us. There was no one, at least not anyone that I could see at the time. Dani, on the other hand, had seen it. I looked around, but there was no one there.

Not surprisingly, Danni slept with her mother that night. I stayed awake most of the night attempting to catch a glimpse of whatever attacked me. Eventually, I succumbed to sleep and passed the remainder of the night on the floor of Danni's bedroom.

The next day, I knew it was time to ask some questions of my oldest. When she returned home from school I approached her.

"Sometimes it is just a feeling of being watched, and sometimes there is actually a black shadowy thing" she responded to my question.

"For a few weeks" she answered the next one.

"It's getting worse" she volunteered, without my asking another question.

"Why haven't you come to me or mom about this?" I asked.

"I don't know" she said. "What would I say to you anyway? I kind of just try to block it out whenever something happens."

"Have you been touched like I was?" I followed up.

"No, this was the first time I have seen it with the lights on and it has never touched me" she said, looking me in the eye for the first time in this conversation.

I was relieved to hear the last part. The thought of me being the only one touched by this thing was somehow weight lifting for me. What was causing this? Was this the source of her behavior changes? I had noticed changes in Dani's behavior recently. Not a lot at one time, but escalating instances that seemed to be occurring more often.

Even though I was still partly in denial, I had to learn more about what we were going through. I also knew I needed to discreetly inquire about such instances or feelings with Abby and Carrie.

So I spent the next few days and sleepless nights trying to research anything that might explain this type of event. Muscle spasms, mass hallucination, stroke, immediate localized gravity failure, anything I could think of. I Googled and Binged and Yahooed any and every natural occurrence I could think of. Most of the searches returned something, but none came back with anything that matched up with or explained what I experienced. So, eventually, I began looking into the last option I could think of, the paranormal, ghosts and etc. Not surprisingly, there were lots of explanations and theories on that stuff on the internet.

Doppelganger didn't seem to fit. Why would I come back and assault myself? Or would that be going forward? Anyway, it couldn't be that because that would be too confusing to be realistic.

Astral projection from a different alternative universe? Really?! Like those people in that universe don't have anything better to do! "Hey, I can transport myself to a different reality; I think I am going to go slap someone in the back of the head and then run." They should be able to do that in their reality.

Poltergeist? Now this seemed to make the most sense, based on what I was reading. As much sense as the whole situation could make, that is. And so that is where I landed, planet poltergeist. This was going to be the theory I ran with, but like I said earlier, only partially correct.

In addition to the research, I began to casually ask probing questions of Abby and innocent inquiries to Carrie. Abby didn't seem to have anything remotely ominous to report. Her only concerns were of household chores and cleaning not being delegated or followed up on. She certainly hadn't been accosted by any unseen forces or felt any unseen eyes on her.

Carrie, being the youngest in the house, needed to be treated much more delicately. Even though she was my conniving child, she was also the one I held my breath with. I had a tendency to worry more about her even before the beginnings of this situation

"Hey baby." I would begin.

"Have you met any new imaginary friends recently?" I asked.

"No daddy" she answered with a giggle.

"You're silly" Carrie added as she bounded up the stairs away from me to her room, several stuffed animals in hand. That told me all I needed to know. The occurrences were confined to Danni and me.

My personal decision to actually think this whole situation was possible was in direct conflict with my religious beliefs. I was raised in a Southern Baptist family. You know the type, church on Sunday morning, Sunday night and Wednesday night and the rest of the week sprinkled with small to medium sized sins here and there. The whole "do as I say not as I do" thing. Even with that going on around me, I decided to embrace the basis of Christianity and its teachings and live right.

My parents saw fit to enroll me in a private Christian school in kindergarten and I spent most of my elementary years there. I learned of God's grace and the gift of eternal life through his son, Jesus. This foundation would be solid and strong, right up until my parents decided it was time to send me to public school. I was completely and totally unprepared for this alien world. I quickly learned that innocent actions like sticking your tongue out at someone would actually be taken as a challenge to someone's manhood and would be met with near instant violence. Yep, I learned that lesson on the very first day of public school, with a good old fashioned playground beat-down.

I knew when I died I was going to Heaven with everyone else that had been saved, but I had never spent a lot of time thinking about the details of life after death. I believed I would see all of my family, and the few friends that had died up to that point in my life, once I got up there. The details of that timing, however, never really crossed my mind. I never even thought to ask anyone questions such as "when I die, am I going straight to Heaven or will I have to hang around here for a while?" There are a lot of devils in those details, among other things.

After the unexplainable occurrence in Dani's room the following days were mostly uneventful. Sure, there were little things that may or may not be able to be explained away. There were little noises at strange times of the day or night or an occasional cold spot, all things that internet sites will tell you are sure signs of paranormal activity. But nothing really that you couldn't just say "that's normal" to and move on. Perhaps it was because, in reality, I was still refusing to believe in this craziness. Therefore, as I walked around in denial, there was no emotion to feed the spirit lurking just beyond our vision, but as with all families, especially those with children, there would soon be some emotions flying about.

The emotions would come in the form of a seemingly small blowup between Dani and me. She had come home from school in a bit of a mood due to something that I couldn't quite figure out. There was no doubting the severity in her mind however and as I attempted to talk her down from the proverbial ledge she continued to get more frustrated and angry. And in turn, this made me angrier. Temper control was not a specialty of mine or my oldest offspring's. It was like throwing gas on a smoldering camp fire. Suddenly, I felt a shudder throughout the house. And then there he was, or rather, it was. We were no longer alone. I could feel it.

As we argued in the living room, feelings of dread and loathing suddenly filled the room. As the entity began to take shape I could actually feel its presence growing. At first I didn't link the appearance of this monstrosity and the horrible feelings surrounding it. But neither was in the room before this confrontation between Dani and I began and as the shadowy figure drew nearer to me the feelings became stronger.

You may think you know what you would do in the event an intruder came into your home. I'm sure you have probably boasted that you would "kick their ass" or "put a bullet in their head", both of which I was fully prepared and capable of doing. But I guarantee you've never planned for a dark shadowy mass taking the shape of a human out of thin air right in front of you. Nope, I know you haven't prepared for that event and neither had I. If it ever does happen to you don't be ashamed if you pee just a little. No shame in that, it would be expected.

The denial was quickly wearing off now. The dark mass moved right past me and toward Dani. I was frozen in fear and shock. Dani stumbled backwards. As she fell back I noticed something new in the figure, details. There was a face. I could see dark hair. And the hands became clearer as they reached for my oldest daughter, who was now oozing fear and it was being quickly absorbed by this monstrosity. In fact, I could almost see the emotion flowing from her to him. The more she freaked out, the more clearly it materialized. Then I reacted.

As the thing's hands stretched out, about to make contact, I lunged. Just like I would have done against any other intruder in my home I jumped and swung my right fist wildly. What else could I do? I never dreamed this would have an effect on the thing, but it did. I actually made contact. The face I saw materializing in profile shuddered with the impact. My desperate punch had landed with a loud smack on his cheek. I actually could see some reaction on the face. The look was one of surprise and then pain.

The thud was quite audible on our oak floor. Everything seems to echo louder when you have hardwoods. The thing that had only seconds before been stalking my daughter was now sprawled across the living room floor. And he was looking up at me in shock. I, on the other hand, was supremely pissed. At the time I didn't know that my anger was actually helping him. He stood, looked at me for a second and then began to come at me. Yep, there was no denying it now; I was in a fist fight with a ghost.

When his first punch hit me I have to admit I was surprised. After all, he was a ghost. However, his was not much of a punch, more of a slap which flopped harmlessly on my shoulder. At the time I really didn't stop to think why my punch landed and his was so weak. After a few more futile swings he began to fade slightly so I reached out to grab him. My right hand grasped his left and I clasped his throat with my other hand. Yep, there was no denying this either, I was now holding on to a ghost.

Before I could react further, he began to melt. There were little holes appearing throughout him as he degenerated into a dark soupy mass that evaporated on the way to the floor. As the holes grew, he disappeared. He dissolved right there in my hands. Then he was gone, nothing was left not even the liquid. I slumped straight down onto the couch which, thankfully, just happened to be right where I was standing. Dani got up and ran to me. It was over.

Later that night, Dani would tell me that she never saw anything other than the dark mass. That she didn't hear the punch's impact or the splat of the thing across the floor. And she had not seen what this thing dissolved into. For Dani, it was there with me one second and just gone the next. Okay, the denial was gone now, but it was replaced with doubt. Had I just imagined my tiff with the thing? And why was it unable to hurt me when just a few days before it was able to push my head down? Was I just making up some of this stuff in my head? On the other hand, I couldn't have imagined the fatigue I was experiencing. My body was completely drained like I had worked out in the sun all day without any water. I was spent and confused.

Dani and I agreed to not speak of this to Abby or Carrie. There was no way we would be able to get them to believe us anyway. So the great cover-up began; dad's fight with the ghost. Only two souls would know about this. Well, three really, but I have no idea who the third would be able to tell.

Things were calm for a few months after the incident in the living room. Dani and I didn't speak about it, even to each other and we definitely weren't going to say anything to anyone else. But things had definitely changed, especially for me. At first, the world just felt somehow different, very soon though, it was looking very different as well. I mean literally looking different.

Like everything else with this crazy ride I was on, the changes began slow and then just exploded. Shadows seemed to be lurking in my peripheral vision, appearing, spying, prowling and then disappearing. I would turn my head to look at what I thought was a person or an animal or just movement around me and there would be nothing there. And then one day, the shadow was still there when my head turned to look.

I was in the back yard raking and just kind of enjoying the beauty of an early fall night. Fall had always been my favorite season. The changing of the leaves, the cleanness of the air and the cooler temperatures all added up to a long standing love affair. So, when it came time to rake the falling foliage, I really didn't mind.

Just like my first ghostly encounter in the living room, the form began shadowy and dark. A black mist formed, hovering at first and then moving, moving towards me.

"Dad gum it, not again," I thought to myself.

But the feelings with this one were much different than the first. Instead of threatening, this presence felt almost benevolent. I didn't feel the need to go after this one. Instead, it felt as if it were coming to me in a calm unaggressive manner.

"What do you want?" I screamed at it. "I thought we already settled this?!"

"Don't think I won't kick your ass again," I half-heartedly threatened. Not wanting to reveal my true level of concern. But at least I didn't pee a little bit this time. Not yet anyway.

The fog tightened into a shape. The shape was human. Holy crap, the shape was that of a woman.

And then the details formed. It was as if all of this person's atoms were swirling around in a windstorm and then began clicking into the correct place. The fog mist became a person in front of my very eyes.

She was an older woman; in her late fifty's perhaps. Her hair was long and pulled back to the back of her head. I could not tell what her hair color was because she didn't have a lot of color to her. She wasn't in black and white like an old picture you would see in your grandparent's house, but she wasn't in color either. It was a sad dullness of browns and grays. Her face was pleasant. Not smiling, but not melting away or gross like Hollywood would probably have you see. And she really didn't look like she wanted to eat me or anything so I guess the whole zombie thing can be dismissed as well.

Her clothes seemed out of place for today. Her shirt had buttons all the way up the front and ended in a simple collar and her dress covered most of her legs. The shoes were still coming together molecularly I guess and I didn't pay much attention to them. At this point she was standing about five feet away from me. We kind of looked each other over to feel one another out. I was absolutely befuddled at what she was going to do and I guess she was trying to figure out my intentions as well. Then her mouth opened.

She was speaking, or making the movements of speech, but I couldn't hear anything. I could not tell what she was saying and I asked her to repeat herself.

"What?" I asked. The words were mouthed again, but I still could not hear her. Her look changed after I shrugged my shoulders and pointed towards my ear. It changed to a look of concern and confusion. At this point I noticed any fear I had previously had gone. I also noticed she was becoming less vivid. She was beginning to slightly blur again, like little pieces of her were coming off and blowing around her. She looked to her right, as if she was being urged on by someone unseen. I looked in that direction but the waning daylight was hiding any other misty people in the shadows of the trees and shrubs of our backyard. When I looked back at her, she was moving forward, right at me, her face now holding a look of determination.

"No, "I yelled as I back peddled, tripping over my rake. I fell. My butt hit the ground and she lunged over me. As I looked up, she dissolved. She was gone. I was scared again.

At that point, Abby came out onto the deck to check on me.

"Are you okay" she started. "And what are you screaming about?" she asked.

"I tripped over my rake," I answered. That was all of the truth she needed to hear. What was I going to tell her anyway?

"Dinner is ready, come and eat" she stated as she walked back into the house. Not surprisingly, I wasn't very hungry at that point. But at least my shorts were dry.

Abby and I met while we were both still at Berry College. I was instantly smitten by her. But she was not so enamored with me. Perhaps because I was infatuated with almost every girl I met in school, either for a moment or several months. Abby knew this about me when we met as the college we attended was not a large one.

Tucked into a valley in the foothills of the Appalachian Mountains, Berry was a picturesque school. It was located about a two hour drive northwest of Atlanta and was just distant enough to feel like you had gone away to college, but still close enough to home for a trip back for necessities. The buildings on campus were all encased in granite and marble from the surrounding mountains of North Georgia and they gave you the feeling of being in Pennsylvania or some other small town in the North rather than deep in the South. The campus was huge and contained thousands of acres of woodlands and fields along with the college's buildings and dormitories. Everything was connected by long winding roads or tree shrouded paths and many a student had fallen in love with the grounds and spent an extra semester or two there just to extend their time in this beautiful place.

On campus everyone either knew everyone else personally or knew of them. It was here which I garnered the reputation of being anti-committal, among other things. Winning over Abby had taken some time as she always seemed to be suspicious of my intentions. Our friends described us as the "two biggest fish in a small pond". They all seemed to be pulling for us and our budding relationship and many of them were directly responsible for the eventual success of it. It did not come easy, however. Both of us tested the other's will and sincerity numerous times. Through all of the head games and stubbornness, eventually the spark lit and began to grow. After dating on and off for several years and in spite of some very emotional breakups, we embraced the obvious and decided to get married.

We had grown as close as two people could since tying the knot and Abby always claimed it was due to my growing up emotionally. I, on the other hand, chalked it up to having a lot of practice relationships which allowed me to hone my skills. Yet, she knew absolutely nothing about what I was going through now. I was not about to tell her, either, not yet anyway.

I was terrified at the thought of attempting to explain the past week or so to anyone, let alone Abby. Even though I completely trusted her, I didn't trust that she would still consider me sane. Perhaps she would think the pressure of constantly failing to find a job had finally gotten to me and I could no longer handle it. Then what would she do? Maybe I was sheltering her. After all, she might become a target of these things if I brought her into the fold. This was completely untouched ground for our relationship and I wasn't sure we were ready for it. I was all about improving our communication, but this was too much. So, I kept it to myself and in my mind justified it as protection.

"Please go to him. He can't do anything else without us"
"Okay"

To this point, I was completely sure of one thing. Something was very different in my life and I hoped it wasn't my losing touch with reality. My body had even begun to change. My appetite had slowed and I wasn't craving the sweets that I usually indulged in. In addition, my physical appearance had started taking on a different look. Overnight, I began to lose the weight I had picked up from sitting on my butt for the past year. I had even begun to add some muscle. But I wasn't working out or even exercising at all.

Throughout my life, I had always been an athlete. It seemed like any sport I wanted to try came easily and naturally to me. I played them all, but most of the gravitational pull of my sports love was towards football. The aggression needed for football seemed to be part of my DNA. At any time, I was able to dial up the emotion and hostility I needed to make a play. It was one of the aspects of my athletic makeup that allowed me to succeed. So much so, that I was given a football scholarship to Berry.

All of that football came with untold hours in the weight room and I had long ago burned out on the act of lifting weights or exercising. Yet, here I was becoming nicely cut and looking very similar, body-wise, to what I looked like right after college. All of this was happening without my lifting, pushing or pulling anything.

Life continued to roll on for me. The job search had become almost counterproductive, but I continued to look. At the same time, I was toiling in house work and cooking, neither of which were coming easy. However, I gave it a valiant effort, whenever I really felt like it. The one chore I was good at was running errands. I had no problem driving around town to take care of the family and household needs.

It had been just over a week since the lady spirit, or hallucination, had visited me in the back yard. Not a day went by, since then, that I didn't think about the exchange between us. In my heart it continued to trouble me as I constantly felt I had let her down somehow. I had decided if anything similar occurred in the future I was not going to handle it in the same way. After all, I had faced some very scary individuals on the football field and in dust-ups in bars throughout my life, so I wasn't about to allow myself to be taken aback again.

As I started the car to head to my next stop on the errand list, I replayed the event in my mind yet again. Only this time, with my new found resolution, I was able to stand my ground and attempt to find out exactly what the lady needed from me. The daydream had gone on for only a few seconds when it completely went awry. In the daydream, the lady had informed me she needed me to apply for a particular job at a local restaurant. With a quick shake of my head, I ended the contemplation, not thinking any further about it. Ahead, the light in the intersection turned red.

I sat in the car staring blankly ahead, waiting for the light to change, with crazy thoughts racing through my head. Was I delusional? Were the things I was seeing hallucinations? And why was my appearance changing? Well I wasn't too concerned about that.

I think I read somewhere one time everything I had been experiencing could be chalked up to a stroke or psychosis, neither of which was appealing. The light turned and I moved into the intersection.

"You aren't psychotic" a voice replied answering my last question.

"Holy crap!" I said looking around to find out who was in my car. In my rear view mirror was my answer; there was a woman in the backseat of my car.

I quickly pulled the car over to the right, entering the first parking lot I could find. Slamming the car into park, I fumbled to unlock the door to make my escape from my would-be carjacker. As I opened the door to get out a sense of calm overcame me. A knowing, if you will. I sat there for a moment with the door open, my escape right in front of me, but I didn't run. In my mind, I knew this wasn't a carjacker. I don't know how, I just knew. I rotated my legs back forward in the seat and shut the door. As I did this I realized the woman was no longer in the backseat. She was in the passenger seat, right next to me. I jumped a little. Well, I jumped a lot. She smiled wryly while looking directly down at the floor of the car as if she were trying to conceal her obvious amusement.

The car was silent for a moment except for the radio. I slowly reached up to turn the volume down. I really wasn't in the mood for the

Kenny Chesney song on the radio at that point. There was complete silence for another moment until her voice interrupted it.

"Aren't you going to ask me who I am or why I am here" she asked.

"I already asked that," I answered. "Can't you read my mind?"

"Nope" the woman answered.

"Then how did you know I asked myself if I was psychotic?" I countered.

"Because you said that out loud" she answered.

"Oh," I responded, slightly embarrassed. After the past few weeks, I felt somewhat prepared for this event

Like every other kid, I had always been interested in ghosts growing up. But as I got older I believed less, even though I was still entertained by the whole concept. Now, rarely did we, as a family, miss the opportunity to watch Ghost Hunters or Ghost Adventures or the random scary movie on cable. Those shows are just too entertaining and it is so easy to make fun of characters in scary movies and their exceedingly stupid decisions.

At one point as a young child, I even had my own unexplainable experience. It occurred in the home I grew up in and I have never forgotten it. On that particular evening, my mom had put me to bed at the normal time. I could still hear the television in the living room as I stared at the open door across the room from my bed. My eyelids seemed to get progressively heavier and I remember closing them for an undetermined amount of time. My next memory was my eyes slowly opening and there at the door was a young girl. Actually, it was as if she were being projected on the door.

Her hair was fair and looked artificially curly with concentric ringlets on either side of her face. She wore a frilly dress which seemed to have a purple or blue stripe at the bottom. I don't remember if she was trying to speak to me, but she was definitely looking at me. I screamed for my father. After I did this she did try to speak to me. I never heard her voice, but I could read her lips and understand her feelings. She was shaking her head and saying "No", her hands beginning to rise with her palms facing me as if to convince me she was not a threat. My dad came through the doorway and she immediately vanished. Whether she was a dream or not she never appeared to me again. One thing I am still sure of, even to this day, I felt bad for calling my dad. Even if this was some weird dream, I still felt like I let her down somehow. Just like the lady from the backyard.

Nothing even remotely similar to that event had happened since. That is until that night in Dani's bedroom and since then there seemed to be no stopping them. In fact, they seemed to be accelerating. And now I was parked in my car looking at a woman who had just appeared out of thin air. Oh yeah, I can't wait to hear this; whatever this may be.

The tension in the car was high. Well, at least my tension was high. The stranger in my passenger seat seemed to be at ease with the whole situation. A few more moments passed and I finally began to put together the words that I wanted to come out.

"So, who are you?" I asked.

"My name is Amy," she answered.

"Why are you here?" I followed up. "Do you have some unfinished business I need to help you with?" Suddenly I had become the Ghost Whisperer.

She laughed. It was a genuine amused laugh. Great, I thought to myself. Nothing like having a ghost make fun of your questioning her!

"Unfinished business?" she said sarcastically. "You don't need to help me with anything. I am here to help you."

"Me?" I answered stunned. "What do you mean help me?" I followed.

"I am here to help you with your transition," she said.

"Transition, what transition?" I countered. "Did I die? Am I dead?"

The concern in my voice escalated as I looked over my shoulder back towards the intersection I had moments before driven through. I half-heartedly expected to see a horrible accident scene that involved my car crumpled up against another car and me or pieces of me hanging from the stop light. To my relief, the intersection contained no such horror.

"No, you aren't dead," she answered.

"Then what am I transitioning to?" I asked, wondering in my mind why I was having to work so hard to get these obvious questions answered with something of more substance than a couple of words.

"It is time for you to begin your calling," Amy volunteered. At that point, I was all ears and I am sure my mouth was wide open, too.

"God has a job for you and I was sent to guide you," she added flatly. I was flabbergasted. How exactly does one reply to a statement of that level anyway?

"We need to go," she said suddenly.

"Go where?" I answered, surprised at how quickly our conversation had turned.

"We have somewhere to be," she responded.

"Wait a minute, I'm not going anywhere until I get some questions answered," I shot back at her.

"You can't just pop into someone's car and start giving orders and expect them to just obey!"

"If I can just pop into your car, I can definitely make you *do* something if you want to argue," she countered, very seriously with a smile that could best be described as smarmy.

"We have to go, how about we drive and we have Q & A at the same time?" Amy offered.

"Fine," I relented.

In my heart and mind, I didn't feel threatened by this woman so I willingly put the car in drive and pulled out into the street. I still had a myriad of questions for her though. Before I could stop myself, the first one flew out of my mouth.

"How the hell did you get in my car?" I blurted.

"Wow, that is your first question?" Amy replied with a laugh.

"Alright, well we have been watching you for a bit so I waited until the exact right time to appear to you," she added.

"Who's we?" I demanded.

"Others like me," she said.

"Like you? And what exactly are you?" I asked.

"A soul, just like you, but a little more… enlightened," Amy said matter-of-factly.

"Enlightened, what does that mean, exactly?" I inquired. "Is that what you mean by my transition?"

"Nope," she answered. "There is still one big difference between you and me," Amy added.

"And what might that be?" I asked sarcastically all the while thinking she was going to say she can just pop into a moving vehicle with the doors locked. I already knew that.

"I'm dead," Amy said matter-of-factly while gazing out the window at the passing scenery.

Nope, that was totally not what I thought she was going to say. I had to force myself to turn away from her and focus on the road in front of me. All the while that smarmy smirk never left her face.

"You are dead?" I muttered.

"Yep, been that way for a while now, well in the sense that you think of dead anyway," she added.

"So you are a ghost," I said. "Why are all of you coming after me now when….."

"I am not actually a ghost, not really," she cut me off. "Not like the two you have met over the past few weeks, anyway."

"Okay, you are being way too cryptic with these answers," I commented.

"So you're a guardian angel then?" I followed.

"Don't flatter yourself, I'm not your guardian angel," Amy responded.

As we drove, I continuously attempted to get a better look at this woman sitting in my passenger seat. Unlike the last spirit I had encountered, Amy was in full color and looked as real as anyone else. Sometimes she would catch me but mostly she would just be looking out the window. She seemed to be fascinated with the backdrop of our drive. Mundane and every day to me, she appeared to be quite interested in the houses and buildings we passed.

Amy was the kind of attractive that snuck up on you. At first glance she was unremarkable; however, as you looked at her the beauty became evident. This definitely wasn't your prototypical ghost.

She appeared to be slightly older than me in appearance, maybe late thirties. Her hair was brown with a slight wave to it and her bangs were held back with a hair barrette. She sported small glasses and had brown eyes that lay just beyond the lenses. She wore jeans and a green and blue stripped short sleeve shirt. This girl looked more like a librarian than ghoul. She even had tennis shoes on. She also began to seem strangely familiar to me; somewhere between déjà vu and vaguely recalling of a passing introduction at a Christmas party.

"Do I already know you?" I asked as I strained to get a better look at her in between stressful glances at the road.

"I don't think so, no," she replied.

"So why did you start watching me?" I continued our conversation.

"Because I was told to," she answered. "Turn right up here," she abruptly added while pointing to a road just ahead. I did as told. What was I going to do, argue?

We had arrived at our destination. It was a house, nothing special or spooky. There was a *For Sale* sign in the front yard and that actually sent a wave of relief over me. I turned to ask my impromptu hitch hiker what we were doing here but she wasn't there. No, she was already out of the car and walking towards the house. Of course she didn't use the door.

"What are we doing here?" I asked.

"I thought we would start you on an easy one," Amy replied, never looking back at me as she strode towards the front door.

"An easy what?" I yelled as I jogged to catch up to her.

"There is someone here that needs your special ability," she answered.

I sprinted to get in front of her and block her entrance into the house. Shooting up the stairs to the front door, I placed my back against the entryway and extended my left arm to block Amy's progress.

"I want to know what the hell is going on!" I shouted turning to face Amy before we entered the house. She wasn't there. I stood there by myself for a second staring down at the red brick stairs in defeat.

"You're already in the house aren't you?" I asked out loud never turning to face the door behind me.

"Yep," Amy's muffled voice answered. "The door is probably unlocked" she added.

I turned around, grabbed the handle and entered the house, feeling completely defeated by the failure of my plan.

"Amy, please tell me what this about!" I begged.

"You are here to help a wonderful lady," she relented with an exuberance that I had not yet witnessed with her. "She is in the house and will likely seek you out as you move through it," she added.

"How does she know me and what am I going to help her with?" I asked.

But my attention was taken away from Amy before she could answer. I was suddenly keenly aware of the hallway that leads away from the foyer. It was almost like a beacon had been turned on and I was tracking it. As I walked towards the hallway opening I noticed a mist forming. It had the same appearance as the others I had seen recently. I continued toward it. The mist solidified into a small woman with plain clothes and a pleasant face. Unlike the lady in the back yard that only seemed to be slightly colored, this lady was almost fully colored. Her clothes were fairly modern and she seemed to be about seventy-five years old. She looked like the typical grandmother. She also looked a little uneasy.

"She is using your fear for energy to materialize," Amy said as she strolled up next to me.

"I'm not scared," I responded.

This was true. I was surprised to realize that instead of being terrified I was extremely excited. I could feel the adrenaline originating in my lower abdomen and shooting outward. Amy turned and looked at me. As I made eye contact with her I noticed she was no longer smirking smarmily. She was looking on in wide eyed amazement.

"Help her go Zach," Amy said.

"How do I do that?" I asked.

"Reach out to her," she responded. "You will know what to do."

As I turned back to face the lady I halfheartedly expected not to see her. But she was there, waiting patiently, just like a grandmother would. The unease was now gone from her face, replaced by a gracious smile. I reached out with my right hand and placed it on her shoulder. I could actually feel the woven rows of her sweater. She placed her hand on mine and looked up into my eyes. After a few seconds, she began to emanate rays of light. Beams of bright white light shot outward from her and filled the room with brightness and warmth. The feeling on my body was one of sitting next to an open fireplace. Just before she completely disappeared into light she said "Thank you". I could barely hear her but I knew by the movement of her mouth what she had said, that and the look on her face. She was happy, at peace and moving on.

I don't remember the walk back to the car. I don't even really remember leaving the house. The feeling, however, was one I will never forget. The only way to describe it was that the feeling surrounding the house was as it should be, in order, peaceful and empty. Once I sat down in the car, I could not move. I was replaying the events of the last few minutes over and over in my mind.

"That didn't look anything like the ghost I touched in my living room the other day," I said, not even sure if Amy was there and listening. She was.

"Yeah, it probably depends on who they are going to meet," Amy's voice responded. "The uglier the soul, the uglier the departure I would imagine."

I started the car and took one last look at the house before I backed out of the driveway. As we drove away, Amy revealed some details about the grandmotherly lady we had just met. She had been a resident of the house we entered for over forty years. She had fallen ill sometime in the past year and died in the house with her family surrounding her. She had led a good life, you could sense it.

"You did good, Zach" Amy said.

"Thanks," I responded.

"Why was she still there, Amy?" I asked. "A grandmother like that should be in Heaven."

"Well, she is now," Amy responded.

With that comment I could no longer control my curiosity. I had too many questions flying about in my head. Just ahead of us on the right side of the road I noticed a neighborhood entrance. I decided to pull off the road and try to get some clarity from Amy.

"Why me?" I asked as I slowed the car to a stop. Amy sat in the back passenger seat looking out the window to her right. She didn't move.

"Amy?" I called out firmly. "Why me?"

"I don't know," she finally answered with strong conviction. She never turned her head, but continued looking out the window towards the wooded area just off the street. Her eyes blinked quickly as if she were flitting from one thought to another.

"So, you're telling me that God just showed up one day and told you to come down here and drop the whole calling thing on me?" I blurted out sarcastically while throwing my hands up in frustration.

That seemed to break her trance on the forest and she slowly turned to meet my gaze in the rear view mirror. No answer came. At that moment I got the distinct feeling Amy wanted to tell me, but wouldn't or couldn't. I wasn't sure which. I lowered my gaze from the mirror and dropped my head in frustration. Seconds later, the car felt different. I checked the rear seat through the mirror again and there was no one there. Amy had disappeared.

I had always been taught, through years of church, Bible school, family talks and any other times the subject came up, when you die you go to Heaven or Hell, based on your relationship with God and Jesus, or lack thereof. I was never quite sure on some of the details, though. You aren't really taught any of that in church or Bible school, not that I remembered anyway.

Now, however, I was very interested in the details of death. Did you move on immediately after you ceased living or did you linger? It sure looked to me like some people were lingering. Or, did your soul take a time out, resting in your body until some high level angel called your soul out of your body as it lay in your casket? Perhaps you just simply moved to a different level altogether and waited for promotion or demotion from there. Maybe the step after death was different for everyone, I really had no idea.

The answer usually depended on who you spoke to and how they felt that day. I remember many instances of aunts or other relatives telling me when I was younger that all my cousins and most other kids were going to Heaven, but I was going to Hell because I was just too mean. I was really good at pissing them off.

That was poorly thought out motivation on their part if you ask me now. At the time, I wore that label like a badge of honor, however. I guess God worked that honor out of me. Over time, I began to realize that the strongest feelings and desires in me were the ones to do good. Not just normal good, but above and beyond good.

There was the time in high school when I saw a police officer who needed help and I stopped to do just that. He had apparently made a traffic stop and was parked on the side of the road behind another vehicle. As I approached, I could see the officer was locked in a hand to hand struggle with another man. I stopped my car in the middle of the road and bolted from the driver's seat in a full sprint. The wrestling match was gaining in intensity as I reached the duo. Just as I got to them the man shoved the officer back, causing him to lose his balance. Before the officer could reengage, I crushed the man with a textbook midsection tackle. I could hear the air rush out of him as we hit the ground. The smile was still on my face as I drove away; having never even spoken to the policeman.

I still wavered back and forth a lot. But over the years as I matured, the tendency to help and love overtook the desire to be bad. I never completely lost the ability to summon my mean streak though. I was just able to hide it well. I also never really dwelled on the details. As I got older I had my faith in my decisions toward my relationships I was building with God and His Son and that was all I concentrated on.

Within a few days of the meeting in the vacant house with the grandmother, Amy returned. I was sitting on the back deck, drinking a mid-morning cup of coffee and suddenly she was there, sitting beside me.

"Coffee smells good," Amy stated.

"Holy crap!" I exclaimed out loud through a spray of coffee drool and spittle. "You have to start warning me somehow when you are just going to show up, Amy."

I was alone at the house during the weekdays so even though momentarily startled I didn't worry when this happened. I was extremely interested in Amy's answers to the many questions that had been constantly filling my thoughts so I was glad to see her. Surely she had some insight into this stuff; after all, she was already dead. We sat silently for a moment, both enjoying the briskness of the air and the many birds flitting from the feeders to the surrounding trees and back.

"Why hadn't that grandmother already gone to Heaven?" I asked, breaking the tranquility.

Amy looked at me, started to answer, and then paused. She looked away and seemed to take a moment to think over her answer before giving it to me.

"C'mon, I can handle it," I added.

"It isn't that simple Zach," Amy countered.

"I don't know the specific reason why she was still in her house, but I can tell you about the complications," she added.

"One of the greatest gifts God gave to us is free choice," Amy began. "It is the major difference between humans and any other creation He has," she said. "He doesn't sit in Heaven and plan every detail of every life that has ever existed, even though He could. We are given choices every minute and He allows us to move through life based on our own decisions. He decides little if anything directly for us, it is we that make the choices that affect ourselves and others."

"You know, I kind of felt like that was the case," I volunteered.

"But what does free choice have to do with the grandmother we met the other day," I asked.

"Just because you die that doesn't mean your ability to make a decision has been taken away," she said. "Try to imagine the level of confusion and fear you will experience at the point you realize you have died? Do you think you will be able to make a good decision?"

"What about the guy from the other day, the very first one?" I asked. "Why was he so aggressive? The others haven't been that way."

"I think you would feel better if you didn't know all of his details Zach," Amy answered.

"That guy attacked me," I countered. "I think I deserve to know why."

"Was he.." I began my next question before Amy interrupted me with further details.

"He was not a good person," she offered. "He preyed on children in life and continued in death. That is how all souls are, you are basically the same after you die as you were when you were alive."

"Great," I responded, feeling much better about hitting him. "I hope it hurt when he melted!"

Amy went on to describe how so many souls either can't decide or make poor decisions at the moment they discover they have died. Many people simply walk the other way out of fear or confusion about what they are seeing or just can't bear to leave their loved ones behind. And the door doesn't stay open for long. Apparently, you have to willingly take a step of faith into this unknown soon after you die.

"This is where people like you get involved," Amy revealed.

"Ever since people have been messing up this process, there has been the need for people like you," Amy said.

"It takes a special person to be able to handle this job," she followed. "You have to possess all the right emotions, understanding, patience and lots of other qualities. Once all of those qualities are evident, God gives you that little something extra."

We continued to talk for a while and Amy revealed more. Mentally, I was back in school and completely engrossed with everything she was telling me. It seems the group that is the most problematic is children. Some simply run and hide and are very hard to find or never reveal themselves in any way. They just linger in the shadows or wander sad, scared and lonely trying in vain to get their families to hear or see them. That made sense.

It was also heartbreaking to think about those scenes. Can you imagine that small innocent soul desperately clutching for their mother to no avail? Never able to actually hold or touch them and unable to make them hear their forlorn cries. And it has been going on for centuries. How can you expect a terrified child to make a leap of faith like that away from their loved ones? I had never even thought about anything that deep, or sad. The thoughts made me sick. I had to think about something else.

"What did you do Amy?" I queried, trying to change my train of thought.

"I guess you could say I took the step," she answered as a blank look overtook her face. She turned her head slightly to the right and seemed to mentally drift away for a moment.

"But many don't."

"What about babies?" I asked.

"How can they be expected to make any decision?" I followed.

"Babies are handled differently, they are assigned to a special group," Amy answered.

She looked away and you could see her mentally racing away to distance herself from this line of questioning. Even though I wanted to press her on the question I didn't. Instead, I decided to back off and take the conversation in a different direction. After all, we were making good progress in our budding, but complicated, little relationship.

"Perhaps we should do a few more move-ons," I quickly asked her.

"Move-ons?" Amy parroted in a mocking tone. "What is a move-on?"

"You know. The thing I do with the touch and the light and…I don't know. What do *you* call them?" I answered back in my own mocking and annoyed tone.

"I don't know. There really isn't a name for the process that I know of," Amy responded. "I will let you work on that."

"You guys need some sort of manual for all this crap," I fired back.

"Yeah, that couldn't hurt," Amy said chuckling. "C'mon we'll go do some more "move-ons," she added using air quotations.

So we would need to head back out. It would be easy to do things during the day. Abby would be at work and the girls at school. At night, it was a bit tougher to come up with alibis. "Going to watch football at Dave's," or "meeting the guys for a beer," were workable standards. But they wouldn't last forever. Abby would tire of that schedule or the girls just wouldn't allow it. They would demand some daddy attention soon. Amy and I had to do the best we could with limited time. I knew eventually there would be no hiding this anymore. Unfortunately, ghost hunting during the daytime is rather tough.

With everyone busy and running around doing things on their schedules there isn't a lot of energy for ghosts to pull from during daylight hours. At night it was easier for spirits to thrive because people weren't as busy and they had more time to get antsy or scared. And the ghosts flourish in this time. Just think, all of those times at night when you had the willies you were justified, you definitely weren't alone.

"Is he progressing?"
"Yes, pretty quickly."

One afternoon, near sunset, Amy came to me as I washed my car. Dani was at cheerleading practice. Abby and Carrie were down the street at a neighbor's house. There would be no need for an elaborate alibi.

"Let's go," Amy announced her presence.

"Damn!" I screamed as I dropped my cleaning brush into a bucket of soapy water. "You gotta start giving me some sort of warning, Amy." I wiped the suds from my face and regained my composure.

"Let me just tell Abby real quick then we can go," I answered.

I shot Abby a quick text and the phone rang almost instantly. The caller ID on my cell announced the caller was Abby. My stomach twisted slightly.

"Hey," I answered the phone as calmly as I could.

"Where are you going?" Abby asked in a stern but quiet manner.

"I have to run out real quick and do a couple of things," I responded. "I won't be gone long."

"Uh huh," Abby responded cynically.

"I won't," I replied. "Love you." I hung up the phone as soon as I heard her answer. My time was running short on keeping Abby at bay and I knew this.

We drove south until the road changed names, a common occurrence in Georgia, and made our way into a small town nestled in the hills and hidden from the back roads. Its name was Taliaferro. I knew of the little town, by name only as I had never been there. As we approached Taliaferro the sunlight began to dim. The high thin clouds which had been present all day were quickly giving way to lower thicker rain producers.

"Rain's coming. Are we going to be inside?" I asked hopefully as I looked up at the darkening sky.

"Yeah, we will probably stay dry," Amy replied.

The town had been a major stopping point along Georgia's main east-west railroad line in its glory days. The wealthy from Savannah and Charleston would make the train trip in the summertime to escape the heat and humidity of the southeast coast. At one time, it even had several respectable hotels which remained full with travelers year-round. But now it was only a shell of its former greatness. The hotels were gone and the structures which remained on the little used streets were either empty or ignored. Amy guided me through the small streets until we arrived at an old tumbled rock driveway blocked by an iron gate. The gate connected a block and stucco wall which surrounded the property we now sat in front of.

"What is this place?" I asked as I peered up through the window at the rusted entrance.

"This was a college many years ago, believe it or not," she answered while also gazing at the entryway. "I'll meet you on the other side of the wall."

I exited the car and walked towards the gate. Immediately, I felt unwanted. The sense of dread was strong and the feelings weren't helping my weak desire to get inside.

Somehow, I wasn't worried about getting caught trespassing on the grounds. In my mind, the most concern I had was what was pushing me away from the other side of the wall. I noticed the random droplets of a light rain beginning to fall and the wind was a bit steadier from the west. It was wind being pushed by heavier rain still approaching us.

"I'm pretty sure the gate is broken," Amy revealed.

"Can't you open it, Amy?" I asked.

"Just climb over," she answered. "I'll meet you on the other side."

"Just climb over," I said in a mocking high pitched manner. "This coming from the woman that doesn't use doors!"

Just down the wall from the gate I noticed a large tree limb hanging down lower than the rest. It originated from an old oak on the other side of the wall and seemed to be placed there for just such a purpose. The athlete in me kicked in and I ran towards the wall, bounding up the side with two strong steps and then leaping upward to grab the limb. I easily pulled myself up and over the wall, landing deftly on the other side.

Amy was walking towards me as I marveled at my feat.

"Pretty good, huh?" I said, looking eagerly to her for appreciation of my act.

Amy only rolled her eyes and turned away, beginning her walk up the path towards the old structure. Her lack of excitement didn't deter me as I knew how impressive the achievement was.

My excitement was now eroding the hesitancy I felt only minutes earlier. I hurried my pace to catch up to Amy and the rain fell a bit harder. As we walked our feet crushed all manner of leaves, limbs and debris scattered along the walkway. Years of springtime storms and harsh winters had deposited a thick layer of organic matter which had no one to clean it up. The continual crunching announced our approach to the base of the hulking stone building.

It reminded me of many of the buildings at Berry. They could have easily been constructed by the same person as they were very similar in appearance. The walls consisted of stacked stone and mortar. The windows were surprisingly still mostly intact. A few panes had cracks or holes, but most remained largely as they had when students looked out through the hazy glass to a world they were hoping to improve by their studies there.

There were three floors above a raised crawlspace or basement; each floor having about ten windows going down its length. The front door was set slightly in and covered by a small feeble attempt at an awning. I feared the awning was waiting for just the right opportunity to collapse and our weight on the stoop might just be that time. The door placed across the opening was obviously not the original and looked very out of place. Someone had apparently tried to put this newer one up in an attempt to keep out the unwanted. Unfortunately, they had forgotten to lock it and after turning the knob, I vaulted over the crumbling stoop and into the interior of the building.

Amy followed me in. She had no fear of any impending awning collapse and strolled right through. Once inside, the foreboding feelings returned to me. This time, they were accompanied by a voice. From somewhere in the building came a shriek of horrifying proportions. It sounded like a mixture of a woman's high pitched scream of terror and dying animal fighting for its last moments. I knew whatever presence I had felt just moments before while outside was almost certainly responsible for that warning shot. The sound was obviously meant to intimidate and would likely be sufficient to clear the structure, on most occasions, of any normal interlopers. Obviously, Amy and I were not normal and we never moved.

I did, however, have to fight through an extreme case of the creeps and did so without allowing Amy to notice the jolt through my body. Verifying this through a quick glance her way, her eyes met mine and we momentarily locked into a stare. Immediately I knew the scream had troubled her as well and she was looking at me to see if I was showing any outward signs of the anxiety rushing inwardly through my veins. It was a standoff.

"What do you want to do, now?" she asked through the stare, probing my current state.

"I'm not gonna lie to you, that was creepy!" I replied, forcing my apprehension to turn to excitement. "Let's go," I added. Amy shot me a knowing smirk and we turned to face the dark.

The inside of the building smelled of dank rotting sheetrock and plaster. Portions of the ceiling were bulging downward with the wear of many a rainstorm. I surmised much of the wet mold smell was originating there and in the adjacent walls. We were standing in a grand lobby. To our right was a doorway, absent the door, which lead down a narrow and dark hallway. The center of the lobby was dominated by a wide marble stairway. Halfway up the rise they separated to the left and right and continued up to the second floor. The marble stairs looked very out of place as their surface still looked grand as every other building component deteriorated. Just beneath each flight of stairs were additional hallways leading away from the lobby. These hallways were much wider than the one to our right but not much better as far as seeing down them.

"Feel anything?" Amy asked.

"Yeah, it's not a good feeling," I answered.

"Well, there is likely more than that one spirit here so don't let it overpower the others," she continued.

She was right. I took a moment to collect myself and discovered other feelings coming to me from different directions. They were subtle and not nearly as strong as the one I had felt outside, but they were definitely there. The feelings given off by the ghosts reminded me of the feeling of someone staring a hole through you. You could feel the sensation and the direction it was coming from and there was no doubt about varying levels of strength. Some of these souls were much stronger than others.

Suddenly, the dark narrow hallway was alive with feeling. There was no breeze within the building, but a sensation of warm air flowing to me from the right was grabbing my attention. It reminded me of the warm breeze you get at night in early summer in Georgia, just after the sun has gone down. I knew instantly this was not the source of the menacing feelings and horrible shriek. Inviting and pleasant, I turned to face whatever, or whoever, was approaching us from the darkness.

At first there was nothing visible, but slowly a column of mist came together as it moved from the hall towards our location at the center of the lobby. My adrenaline levels spiked and this seemed to quicken the appearance of our first ghost of the night. Within two more steps it was fully discernable.

Walking towards us was a man. He wore jeans which looked worked in and frayed and a black long sleeve button up dress shirt which was un-tucked. His face was mostly hidden by a long dark beard and his brown hair reached almost to his shoulders. His appearance fell somewhere between unkempt drifter and grunge rock star. As he approached, I could see a warm agreeable smile appearing through his thick facial hair and piercing ice blue eyes which seemed to soften his overall appearance. He was actually rather young. Too young to sport the beard he wore, anyway. I returned the grin and decided to

take matters into my own hands by not waiting
on Amy to coach me through this one.

"Hello sir, my name is Zach and I am here to
help you," I greeted him as I moved to shake
his hand.

Behind me Amy snickered. I suddenly felt
as if I was standing on a deserted island of
stupid. As I listened to Amy giggle I noticed
the man looking at me as if I had just told him
I wanted to cut and sell his beard. By this time
he had stopped just short of my arm's length
and stood with his hands in his pockets, still
smiling.

"Here to help me, nah, I think I'm here to
help you son," the man answered my greeting.
"Hello Amy," he added as he glanced past me.

Now I felt stupid *and* was completely confused.
Amy peered over my shoulder to greet the man with
the warm smile of longtime friends, completing
my tumble into embarrassment.

"Hey James," she said with a wave.

Turns out, James wasn't a drifter, but a
preacher. He had traveled all over the South
back in the 1930's spreading the Word of God
with traveling revivals and impromptu roadside
sermons. He was revered and loved by thousands
as a true man of God who actually lived what
he preached, a rarity then as now. He had the
popularity of a modern rock star or athlete
in the early 20th century church centric Deep
South, right up to the night he died.

"Yep, drove right off the side of a mountain
just outside of Anniston during a mean
thunderstorm," James told me after Amy had

begun the story of his life. "My body is still there, they never found it."

"Why haven't you gone on to Heaven?" I asked with childlike curiosity.

"'Cause I'm a preacher, I can still lead souls to God," he answered with a wise smile. "Maybe even better now than when I was alive. It's definitely easier."

I nodded in acceptance.

"Oh, I'm sure I'll go home one day," James continued. "Just not right now."

His smile was contagious and welcoming. It was impossible not to be enamored by this man. He spoke to you as if he had known you for years and always looked me straight in the eye for an emphasis which was unneeded. His words carried great sincerity and weight. James had been guiding souls to this abandoned school for generations. It was a rendezvous point for spirits needing to go on. Once here, they would await someone like me.

"You are the first chosen person I have seen in a while," James revealed to me. "There used to be a lot more of your like, but not anymore. Oh, there would be an occasional one pop up from time to time, but they almost always quit, give up or get…"

"Well, we're here now," Amy interrupted before James could finish.

"Get what?" I said curiously, even though I knew what he was going to say.

"Right! Look you two; there are quite a few souls in here tonight," James informed us. "Some I have sent here and some I have not. You need

Terry L. Kemp

to be careful with a couple of these folks son, they aren't really nice."

James facial expression changed at this point and I knew exactly what he was talking about. The intimidating scream directed at us when we entered had to be from one such spirit. I was feeling unsure of myself at this point as I wasn't sure how I would handle a confrontational ghost. I was thankful to have Amy guiding me through any impending encounters and when James told us he would be hanging around for a while as well I was even more grateful. I would not be alone in this.

We decided to go up to the second floor as this seemed to be the origination point of multiple streams of feelings for me. Other than the splatter of light rain on the rotting roof, the building was quiet as we ascended the marble stairs. As we climbed, our surroundings became darker as there were no sources of light anywhere. Once we reached the landing for the second floor everything seemed to change. There was a sudden rush of emotions and even though the structure remained silent of noise there was a storm of feelings flying all about.

"Amy, I can't see anything up here" I whispered into the darkness. "Should I get the flashlight out of the car?"

"Nope," Amy answered. A warm feeling began to emanate from just behind my right shoulder. This was quickly followed by a comforting glow which quickly surrounded us. It reminded me of the glow from a candle only without the flickering.

"Pretty good huh?" Amy gloated while sporting a proud smile.

I rolled my eyes and turned away in an effort to get her back for not appreciating my bounding the outside wall moments earlier. Her trick was much better than mine but I wasn't about to let her know that.

The light Amy was now providing lit up the hall nicely. Directly in front of us a ghost materialized as he fled down the hall, disappearing into a room at the end. I could now feel several spirits close by. My heart began to race with a mixture of excitement and fear. To our left a spirit emerged from a doorway. It was a girl and she looked to be about twenty five years old. Her blonde hair was held back by a red ribbon and she was clad in a modest white dress. She seemed eager and timid at the same time as she approached our trio.

"It's okay," James soothed her and she seemed to relax a bit. "This is Zach. He is one of the folks I told you would eventually come to help you."

"Hello," I said. "Are you okay?"

"Yes, I'm fine," the girl answered. "Just really nervous."

"Don't be nervous, you have a lot of loved ones waiting on you. They will be so glad to see you," Amy injected.

With that statement she moved toward me. I reached for her hand and she grasped it with both of hers. Her hands were warm to the touch and this surprised me. I fully expected to feel only an icy grip. As she stood in front of me she caught my gaze and smiled for a second. Then, with a burst of light, she left the old building, and the three of us, to go to a much better place. My hands were instantly cooler and I felt a momentary jolt of electricity which rendered me weaker and slightly numb. I shook off the fatigue and tingle and looked around for our next opportunity. Down the hall spirits would occasionally poke their heads out from rooms. Sometimes I could see their full face and at other times there would be only a feeling of being observed.

"You alright son," James asked.

"Yeah," I answered. "Where to now?"

"You tell us," Amy chimed in. "What do you feel?"

I could still feel several spirits somewhere near. But the feelings were getting weaker. There were no more peeking souls visible down the second floor hall. Hoping to get a better sense of where all our targets were, I took a few steps down the hall and stopped. I was not feeling much. The sensation reminded me of the feeling of water leaving a bathtub as it is drained from around your body. Our ghosts were no longer on this floor.

"They are gone," I said, confused about why they would run from us.

We slowly walked to the stairs and relocated to the third floor. Once there, our pace was slowed by the uneven and rotting floor. Every step was a test of faith; faith that the floor would not fall from under our feet. As we walked down the hall, it became obvious the spirits

I had felt earlier were not on the top floor either. There were no feelings of not being alone and the only sounds in the building were those of our feet on the slightly spongy flooring, punctuated with the occasional squeak of a still firm floor board. Somewhere close by, a clap of thunder was muffled by the sound of the rain which was picking up its pace outside.

"There's nothing up here," I said somewhat frustrated. "The only spirit I feel is James'."

"Where do you think they are?" Amy asked.

"The only place we haven't gone is the basement," James said reluctantly.

"Well that's where we need to go then!" Amy responded confidently.

"James, why are they running from us?" I asked.

"I don't think they are. I think they are being herded somewhere, like the basement," he replied.

"More like pulled," Amy added. "I have seen this before. We will probably find them downstairs in the basement."

I did not share Amy's confidence. To me, the building just felt empty and we were wasting the rest of our time. James no longer looked happy. His feelings were betrayed on his face as he now carried a look of concern. He and Amy knew what was coming, I obviously did not. But I kept walking anyway.

As we descended the marble stairs, Amy and James dodged a few puddles forming due to the rain finding its way inside. I found this amusing as I realized I was the only one of this group which could actually be harmed by a slip and fall. I did let my mind wander for a moment to imagine if these two could even get wet.

We made our way across the lobby and moved down the narrow hall James had emerged from earlier. Halfway down its length was another stairwell. This one was not constructed of marble, but rather wood. It appeared unsafe for any soul, dead or otherwise, to walk down. Amy was suddenly absent and I knew she had gone ahead of James and me. I was stunned to see James begin to make his way down the rickety walkway.

"Keep close to the outside edges," he informed me. "They will still have the most strength."

"Why don't you just pop down there like Amy?" I asked dumbfounded.

"I have to do this just like you do son," he answered matter-of-factly.

I kept the confusion to myself and concentrated on safely getting to the base of this deathtrap. At times I found myself holding my breath. There was no doubt in my mind I was going to plummet through these rotting wet boards. After a few moments of unsteady foot placement and the skipping of missing stair steps, I reached the bottom. The basement was already lit by Amy's presence. This was comforting, until my eyes fully adjusted to the scenery. Her glow revealed a disturbing landscape.

There were few walls left standing. Most had long ago been destroyed by vandals or the incessant seep of weather. Piles of debris and trash littered the poured concrete floor. Scattered among this rubble were the bodies of a few animals in various states of decay along with tattered clothing and shoes. The smell was unbearable and completely overtook my senses. One moment it would be the unmistakable odor of animal urine and then suddenly the smell of rot would overpower it. This was not a pleasant place to be sure.

On the far end of the basement I noticed a doorway. It was partially blocked by some of the floor beams which had fallen in at that point of the building. The door was slightly ajar and rain was freely flowing in through the opening. A large puddle was quickly expanding there. The pool was dark and could have just as easily been blood in the dim light. I fought back the sudden urge to run to the door, fling it open and flee from the basement.

My senses were now picking up multiple streams of feelings. A blizzard of emotions now flew about my body and I had to close my eyes to begin to sort them out. To my right behind one of the few remaining walls, was the closest spirit. Concentrating on this, I moved towards it. Between myself and the wall I needed to get beyond was a pile of debris which I didn't dare step onto. I moved around it and towards the wall. Behind the wall was impenetrable darkness. I could feel the spirit move away from me and into the far corner.

"Amy, can you come over here?" I asked in a hushed tone. "I can't see a thing."

"Yep," she answered and the shadows from the walls and piles all began to change and move as she approached.

A line of light reached from the wall and crept towards the back corner of the room I now faced. The remainder of the room seemed to take an eternity to lighten and I feared a horrible something would fly out of the darkness and overtake me before I could fully see. The sense of this spirit was now very close to me and I knew I was closer to it than James as he lingered behind us.

Amy's light finally fully arrived, revealing the ghost of a black man not five feet in front of me. He was sitting in the corner with his knees pulled up close to his chest and his head down. His arms rested on the floor by his sides. If I didn't know better, I would have thought him just a dead body sitting there motionless.

Other than a torn and ragged piece of cloth wrapped around his privates and a similar surrounding his feet, he wore no clothes. His body was lean and dirty, his hair unkempt.

"Little man?" James voice questioned from behind me. "Is that you?"

With this question, the man raised his head slightly to reveal his dark eyes. They were filled with tears and fear. He slightly motioned his head up and down in a weak effort to signal yes to James' question. James walked forward, past Amy and myself and knelt at the side of the man. He placed his hand on the man's head and slightly rubbed it. To me, the gesture appeared to be one of a father to a child. A reassuring touch and loving rub to let someone dear know you cared and were there for them.

"This here's Little Man," James revealed with a relieved look on his face. "I met him years ago in my travels around these parts."

"As a preacher?" I queried.

"No, as a ghost" James replied. "I never thought he would make it here, but he did. Stand up Little Man, it's okay."

James guided the man to his cloth wrapped feet. As he rose I was taken aback by his height. It seemed to take him a full minute to completely unfold and stand to his true stature. Once erect, Little Man stood nearly six inches taller than my six foot three frame. He was huge. But something about this spirit was different. Although a man stood in front of me his soul didn't seem to match his body. His gaze and facial expressions were of someone much younger.

"He's different, isn't he?" I asked of James.

"Yes, he is," James began. "He has the mind of a child, maybe six or seven."

Little Man nodded in agreement as James continued to steady him and hold his hand. The years of shame and mistreatment of this man came through his soul and at me like a water cannon. I felt it striking me and freely flowing down my entire body. I found myself not wanting to know what all he had been through. This would have been debilitating to me. My strongest desire was to get this soul to a better place.

"Little Man, do you want to go see your family?" I asked him, fighting back an overwhelming mix of emotions.

"Yeah," he answered slowly with a childlike voice. "Th th th they with God, I kn kn kn know that much."

"They miss you," Amy chimed in.

"Ya th th th think s s so" Little Man responded.

"I know so," Amy answered with a confident smile. The sight of this smile found me unprepared. To this point in our fledgling relationship, the only smiles I had witnessed were generated at my expense.

"But I th th th think that man gonna be m m mad at m m m me," Little Man said as he looked down at James.

"What man?" I asked.

"Th th th that m m mean m m man," Little Man answered in a childlike whisper, as if he didn't want someone to hear. "He right over th th there."

I have always heard people speak of getting goose bumps. Until that moment, I had rarely experienced them. I had felt fear and been awestruck by emotional situations such as this, but never have I had my skin raise and hairs stand on end until that moment. A tense silence fell over the four of us. Amy and I looked around in an attempt to see what Little Man was talking about. Instead of feeling scared, as I probably should have, I became very focused. The challenge of meeting a mean spirited spirit fired me up. James, however, knew it was time to get Little Man out of there.

"Little Man, take Zach's hand!" James stated with a sudden sense of urgency.

"It's okay," I said as I took the man's hand and prepared for a strong handshake back.

Instead I received a hug of immense proportions. Little Man's embrace lifted me from the ground and my feet dangled. My lungs struggled for oxygen as he squeezed inwardly. This man had no idea of his strength. Just before unconsciousness, Little Man's grip disappeared from my body. The foul basement was temporarily filled with the whitest light imaginable, and then returned to its dank atmosphere. My feet landed with a muffled thud on the trash littered floor.

"Whoa, you okay?" James asked me as Amy helped me to my feet.

"Yeah, I'm fine," I answered as I brushed the dirt and wetness from my clothes.

Instinctively, I smelled my hands to ascertain the amount of nastiness attached to them from being on the dirty floor of the basement. They smelled much like the air surrounding us.

"Uhh, gross," I mumbled.

"Let's see if we can find this soul Little Man was talking about," Amy requested.

"Yeah, he acted like he was pretty close by," James added.

"He is," I admitted to the others. "I can feel him."

As we turned from a narrow passage into a room closer to the rear of the basement the space was suddenly filled with an air of foreboding and apprehension. It felt as if a curtain had been drawn around the three of us in an attempt to hide something. I continued deeper into the

room to effort finding the source. I wasn't sure
if this could be the other spirit Little Man
had just spoken of but whatever it was carried
a foreboding presence.

I found I could follow the feeling like a
scent. Outside, another low grumble of thunder
punctuated the mood. Suddenly all of my senses
were awake. I could hear the drip of the
rainwater as it poured in the basement door
intermingled with the crunch of only God knows
what under my feet. My eyes were now keenly
aware of a dark pulsating form at the far corner
of the basement. The glow Amy was providing
us helped to illuminate the area slightly. As
we approached the corner, the mass remained
dark as the rest of the area brightened. I
was now within feet of the dark cloudy form.
My adrenaline pulsed upward and my excitement
driven anxiety climaxed. I was almost on top
of this thing.

From the center of the mass a face began to
emerge. I stopped. Amy and James now flanked
me. Whatever this was, we had it backed into a
corner. By the time the old adage of never back
a wild animal into a corner came into my mind,
it was too late. The animal sprung.

The face completely formed and stretched
grotesquely out of the now churning black mass,
connected by a thin neck. There was little hair
on its head, only long scraggly patches here
and there. The eye brows were missing as were
its teeth. From the mouth a dark liquid flowed
and ran the length of the chin, dripping to the
ground directly in front of me. James gasped.

Amy stood undaunted, her legs slightly bent at the knee, prepared for whatever was to come. I was too shocked by its vacant black eyes to know how to stand or even what to do. Was I supposed to touch this thing? My instincts told me to punch it as hard as I could.

"Get out!" it said with conviction. The black liquid sprayed from its thin lips as it spoke. I stepped back to prevent the vile spray from touching me. No one else moved. We were in a standoff.

Our delay in reacting to the monster's request only seemed to anger it. This didn't surprise me in the least. From out of the dark mass an arm connected to a torso revealed itself. Seconds later the other arm became visible and then the legs, as it fully revealed itself. All of its limbs were gangly. As it stood directly in front of me, I found myself curious how these skinny legs were holding the thing up.

Instantly, one of the long skinny arms flailed outward at me. The top of my head sustained the impact of an open handed slap of some force and I was dumbfounded for a second. This pause was plenty of time for the other hand of this abhorrent creature to reach out and grasp my throat. The muscles in its arm rippled under thin greyish skin as it attempted to squeeze my airway shut.

Behind me I could hear James praying. I could not make out specific words, but I knew the gist of it. I attempted to back away while using both of my hands to push the thing's arm from my neck. My excitement had turned to fear and it was growing as my air lessened.

"Ahem," Amy cleared her throat and moved into my peripheral as she placed her hand on my shoulder.

The touch of Amy's hand was slight. I could barely feel it. But there was no doubting its effect. Like a shot of adrenaline flying throughout my body the power of Amy's touch gave me confidence and strength. I knew I could manhandle this meathead and was now determined to do it. All I needed to do was calm my fear and concentrate on the needs at hand, literally.

My first action was to forcefully remove the skinny hand from my throat. A quick grasp and twist with my right hand was sufficient to accomplish this. The look on this evil spirit's face changed immediately from intimidation to shock. My eyes widened with a surge of surprise and confidence. I felt the corners of my mouth slightly curl upward in an "oh yeah" smile.

It turned its body to flee. This was fruitless as my grip was now locked in. I reached for the back of his head to grasp what little hair he had for leverage. Instead, my handful was of sagging cold skin which seemed to stretch from his head. The elasticity reminded me of the Stretch Armstrong doll I had as a kid. I wondered if he would leak the same pink gel if I continued to pull. I desperately wanted to find out, but I resisted the urge.

As this tug of war was going on something amazing happened. The black mass pulsating directly behind the monster man began to rapidly dissipate. Within seconds, the dark was completely gone. From this area sprung a mass of different ghosts. Before me a mob of souls from many different eras began to scatter through the basement. Some stood nearby to watch the removal of this evil force which had been holding them, but others simply ran, vanishing around corners or out the door. A man and a woman sprinted past me. Two children let out a "hooray" as they ran barefoot around the corner toward the stairs. A man in a timeless looking business suit nodded to me in appreciation before disappearing completely.

"No!" the vile spirit screamed in desperation. Before I could react in anger at what he had obviously been doing, he was gone. No light, no flash only dissolving into dark nothing.

"Thank you God," James commented.

"Nice job," Amy added. Her demeanor had remained cool and collected, just as her adulation for my task completion.

"Well, let me try to go round some of these souls up for you," James stated as he made his way towards the rickety and rotting stairs.

"Okay. We'll talk to any that stayed to watch the show," Amy answered.

It turned out there was only one spirit remaining in the basement and I moved him on without problem. The rest had scattered. I understood. They were free from the control imposed on them by this monster of a soul after countless years. In my mind I said a quick prayer for them and wished them well, knowing I would likely see them again.

James didn't find any more of the souls we had just freed. But he decided to hang around the old structure for a little while anyway, just in case any returned or reappeared. Amy left just before I departed, leaving me to drive home alone. I returned home exhausted, but in time to tuck the girls in and say goodnight prayers. No questions were asked of me and I chalked this up to Devine intervention. I was too tired to lie anyway.

Whenever the time was right, Amy and I would go. Sometimes the trip would be short. At other times, we would have to drive for longer. I would be doing something random around the house. Cleaning out the garage, reading my Bible, watching SportsCenter, and suddenly Amy would be there, usually scaring the crap out of me, always surprising me.

"You aren't ever going to show up when I am in the bathroom are you?" I asked.

"No, and I avoid you when you are in the shower as well," Amy replied.

"Thank God," I answered.

"Yep, thank God," she added.

"I have one for us," she said.

"All right, let's go," I answered with excitement.

I walked through the empty house to the garage and got in my car. Amy was there beside me. We pulled out of the garage and she directed me were to go. The fall sun was beginning to get lower in the late afternoon sky. This had always been my favorite time of year and this was one such reminder. The sunset was going to be beautiful. The western sky was beginning to glow red and yellow and accented the colorful foliage surrounding our drive.

An hour later, we were almost there. We were a good bit off the main highway back in very dense woodland on a dirt and gravel road. The gravel crunched under my tires as we slowly made our way deeper into the forest. The smaller branches and limbs scratched at the car like boney fingers as we rounded each bend in the road. My caution was high. I maintained a slower speed because I knew at any moment something could hurl itself out of the thick overgrowth at us. And then it happened. Without even the wiggle of a branch or the snapping of a twig, a form flew out of the underbrush directly in front of the Tahoe. My reactions were immediate. The only thing I could do was slam on the brakes and control the slide of the vehicle on the thin layer of broken up granite and Georgia red clay.

"Crap, I *knew* that was going to happen," I screamed through clinched teeth.

The form had emerged from the woods on the right and landed about three feet out on the road. My jerking of the wheel to the left had placed Amy's door directly into the impact path as the big SUV lurched sideways. Amy never uttered a sound. She braced herself by grabbing the handle above the window with her right hand and flexing her right leg almost straight. The motion lifted her rear slightly from her seat. She continued to stare out the window as the encroaching object rapidly neared her window.

Amy turned her head away just before impact. With a thump the car collided with the thing blocking our way. As we slid to a stop I saw something being propelled away from us by the impact of the passenger side door. The Tahoe had struck the deer in the best possible place, for him anyway, the butt. It landed on all four feet and bounded into the woods on the other side of the road.

"Six, maybe eight pointer," I remarked as the magnificent animal was swallowed by the vegetation surrounding it. "This time of year those dang things are everywhere and they always seem to jump in front of you at the worst time," I added.

"Great," Amy answered sarcastically. "I hope you didn't hurt it."

I got the vehicle pointed in the right direction and we continued our journey. At the end of the road a pea gravel driveway looped off to the right. There in the center of the semicircle sat an old run down Victorian style home. It had round turrets and big porches. In its time, it must have been a beautiful centerpiece for a well to do family in this part of the state. Now it was sagging and sad. The feelings emanating from the structure matched the visual. As I got out of the car, I was struck with a tidal wave of melancholy. It was as if a warm and cold wind were striking my body and pushing me backwards. You could feel the sadness.

I fought back the urge to get back in the car and cry. I had to control myself, my emotions. Amy had told me ghosts fed on our emotions countless times, and I wanted to make sure I was in control of them. I wanted to control how much nourishing occurred. On the first couple of these excursions I had not been very good at this emotional control. A few times I had given the ghost way too much energy, either by being too scared or too angry. Amy had stepped in and taken control of those situations until I could get it together and do my job. Now, however, I felt I was getting much better at self-control. "Your door is dented where it hit the deer's butt" Amy said with a hint of amusement as she closed the door.

The levity was just enough to allow me to compose myself. I gathered my emotions, straightened my stance and forced back the tears. I walked towards the large front porch which was both aesthetically welcoming and emotionally foreboding. It was an amazing mixture. Up the stairs I went, and arrived at the front door, Amy by my side. I pushed open the door and small flakes of decades old white paint floated down.

"I wonder if there is lead in that old paint," I thought randomly as I walked through the flurry of flakes. The house was dank and dark. It smelled of decades old damp wood with a slight hint of cold dry dirt, like you would find in a crawlspace. The light coming through the windows and the now open door helped my eyes adjust.

In front of us was a large foyer and to the right a large spiral staircase lead up to the second floor. Some of the boards on the floor were missing. Others were covered in leaves and debris or small pools of water. The stairs were mostly still there and oddly the plaster walls were still generally in place.

"Careful where you walk Amy," I said as I turned to look at her. She cut her eyes over at me, raised her brow and slightly turned her head revealing her smarmy smirk. I knew this look well now. It was her way of making fun of me when I said something stupid. Telling a ghost to be careful where she walks definitely qualifies as a stupid statement.

The feelings flowing to me from all over the house were getting stronger. They were all mixed together. A moment of debilitating sadness would be broken by a second or two of glee and innocence. I carefully began to move about the dilapidated structure following the feelings like a scent or warm breeze.

"Any ideas?" I asked Amy.

"Nope, I got nothing," she replied.

"It's almost like they are hiding," she added.

"They?" I asked, pausing for a moment to get better feel. "Oh yeah, I feel that. There does seem to be more than one spirit here."

I mounted the stairs and began to make my way to the second floor. Once I arrived at the top of the flight I realized how much less light there was. Amy made her way up and stood next to me. Realizing the dark was nearly impenetrable, she lifted her hand and immediately the hallway was lighter.

"That is the best I can do," she said.

"That works," I responded.

As I lifted my eyes towards the end of the hall I saw a form. It was dark and appeared mostly solid.

"There we go," I commented.

"Yep, I see her," Amy said.

As I walked down the hall I too saw that the form was a woman. She was small and had her hands together resting across her abdomen, fingers laced. She reminded me of a school teacher from long ago, hair in a bun, long floor length dress and simple white shirt. She was not a very pleasant looking woman and the scowl on her face should have been a tell. As Amy and I moved down the wide hall the lady moved forward to meet us. Approaching her I realized something was not quite right. The feelings I had been following were now being overrun by a terrible force. It was as if my mind could smell something horrible. The feelings reminded me of the night encounter in the basement of the old college. "Uh oh," I thought to myself. "Here we go again."

My head turned slightly in recoil as I stopped in front of the school teacher. Amy could obviously sense this as well as she remained a step behind me, but moved to my left. Then I noticed the light Amy had given us was beginning to dim. Something was terribly wrong. At that very moment I noticed two small children peeking out of a doorway a few more feet down the hall. When I saw them the feelings I had been trailing returned. I smiled at them and them at me. When the school teacher shot a look at them over her right shoulder they disappeared into the room from which they had been leaning out of. And that is when the school teacher looking lady hit me.

She hit me with the force of what felt like a brick. When she struck me, the terrible mental smell returned. I flailed across the hall into a closed door. The door did not remain closed as I smashed through it landing in a sun lit room with peeling yellow wallpaper. The school teacher was right behind me. As I lay in the middle of the floor I could feel a stream of cold sweat roll down from my forehead to my ear. Suddenly, she was leaning over me. I could feel her evil nature pushing at me as she reached down and grabbed my throat.

"You can't have them!" she screamed at me, tightening her grip.

"I have gotten rid of your kind before," she added.

It was now painfully obvious what was going on in this house. This horrible soul had been keeping these two children here for who knows how long, never allowing them to garner the peace and joy they surely craved. Unfortunately, Amy's information wasn't quite complete and my neck was paying the price. And worst of all, I was getting very angry. This anger was like throwing gas on a small fire making it much bigger and harder to control. The lady was obviously feeding off of it and getting stronger. The madder I got, the stronger she became and I couldn't move.

Suddenly, Amy was there. She was standing next to the lady with her hands on her hips like she was disgusted with the whole situation. "Join the club Amy," I thought. Amy rolled her eyes and knelt beside the scrum that was the school teacher and I. "Uh, you are stronger than she is, please act like it," Amy reminded me. As I realized Amy was correct I instantly began to calm myself and gather my thoughts. The teacher turned her head to glare at Amy as she began to lose control of me.

"Yeah, he is!" Amy said to her matter-of-factly while looking her directly in the eye. This allowed me to gather my thoughts and shove the school teacher backwards. I had no remorse for shoving her. As she fell back I stood.

"Send her!" Amy demanded.

I placed a hand on each of the lady's shoulders and began to concentrate on what needed to be done to her. I had to turn my head away as her pungent evil air was very intense at this close range. As she was dissolving, Amy approached her and stuck a defiant index finger in the horrible lady's face, lightly poking her nose.

"You have someone to answer to, they are waiting for you," Amy beamed. And then this awful lady was gone.

The atmosphere in the house changed instantly. The warm feelings I had been surrounded by earlier wafted over me again like an inviting perfume. The two children were now in the room with us. They were each about eight years old, a boy and a girl. They had brown hair and angelic faces. They smiled as they moved to me with the eager innocence of souls barely more than toddlers. I cannot imagine the despair and loneliness and terror of being a child kept in a place against your will by an evil soul for decades upon decades. They each wrapped their arms around me and told me their names.

"I'm Emma," the little girl said with the slight lisp of a young child.

"And I am Ethan," added the little boy with the excited pride which all little boys should have.

I knelt down to them and smiled through a face full of tears.

"My name is Zach," I said. "And this is Amy."

I knew these tears. They were the tears of pure love, unable to be tainted. Children had always done this to me. I could barely even talk when each of my own beautiful girls were born.

"Thank you," they said in unison. Emma reached up with a tiny finger and wiped some of the tears from my cheek smiling at me with the knowing of a soul far older than her appearance.

I wrapped my arms around them and concentrated on helping them go. They began to explode in streaks of light. Amy moved towards us.

"You have lots of people waiting on the two of you," she said with a warm smile.

They smiled, grasped one another's hands and raised their faces upward and then they were gone. The feelings of joy and happiness lingered in the house for several minutes after the children left. Somewhere in Heaven right now a father and mother were reuniting with the children they had not been able to touch in generations. The thought of this meeting was enough to send me over the edge emotionally. Being a father and knowing how much I loved my children, I could not imagine not being able to touch or hug them for as long as those parents had waited. I wept uncontrollably as I felt that father's joy and sadness. I knew what kind of reunion was going on somewhere at that very moment.

"You okay?" I heard Amy ask after a few minutes. I nodded, wiping away the few tears that had not fallen to the old wooden floor boards.

"Okay, c'mon. You're going to attract every ghost in the county with all that crying," Amy said with a reassuring smile. "Let's get out of here before they all show up."

We made our way through the once grand old house and down to the front door. As we exited the house I noticed a van rolling to a stop on the gravel drive directly behind my car. I paused for a moment to think about an excuse for being there, but really couldn't come up with anything believable. Amy was nowhere to be seen by that time. So I just figured I would play it cool and make my way to the car. As I walked towards the car I heard Amy's voice.

"Don't worry, they aren't a problem for us," she said flatly. "Just get in the car."

Three people got out of the van, two men and one woman. All of them on black t-shirts with the same symbol on the front. I could not make it out as I was now hurrying to the car. The driver immediately made eye contact with me as I continued to walk, placing my car between me and them, just in case Amy was wrong.

"Hey," the driver began as he moved toward me.

I fumbled for my keys struggling to get them out of my pocket. The driver continued to move toward me. I noticed he was of small stature with dark hair and dark eyes. By the time he reached the driver side of my car I had stopped taking note of the details about him and was concentrating on getting in the car.

"Are you related to the Jansen's?" he asked leaning down and looking through my partially open window. I assumed they were the family that owned the house we were trespassing in, among other things.

"No, just looking for real estate opportunities," I countered.

"Huh?" the driver started. "I wasn't aware the property was for sale."

"My mistake then," I answered as I started the car.

As I drove away I noticed the other two van passengers unloading what looked like equipment boxes. I assumed they were contractors preparing to do some work on the once beautiful house. I turned the car down the other side of the driveway loop and began to make my way to the road.

"Real estate opportunities?" Amy's voice echoed through the car with a noticeable snicker. She was now in the back seat smiling up at me through the rear view mirror.

"Shut up," I answered through my own smile. "They bought it."

Apparently, we weren't done that day as Amy directed me toward another predetermined location. The sun began to melt into the horizon as we were off to another destination. The drive seemed short as I let the events of the past few minutes roll over my mind. Did I do everything right? Man that teacher lady could really hit hard. What was next?

A few miles later we had apparently arrived as Amy told me to pull off the road and make my way down yet another gravel drive. This was becoming scarily exciting to me. Like treasure hunting or some crazy game of terrifying hide and seek. The adrenaline rush I was experiencing at each of these events was becoming powerful, almost drug like. To this point in my new found hobby, I was already becoming very attracted to the experiences Amy was putting me in. With each successive test I was becoming more enticed by the feelings generated.

It was very dark in the woods off the main road as the sun was now below the horizon. The drive went slightly downhill and turned from gravel to dirt to pine needles and woodland debris. The forest surrounding the drive steadily encroached, the path narrowing from drivable to walk-able. I parked and popped out of the car full of zeal for whatever came next. The trees were huge; they had been there for hundreds of years. Their limbs strained with the weight of uncountable numbers of leaves and limbs and they seemed to be embracing the path we were now heading down.

Soon we entered a clearing bordered by a large creek opposite of where we now stood. I could see two large forms on opposite sides of the clearing through the slowly fading light. One was obviously an old stacked rock chimney. The other was a pile of stones that looked at one time to have been another chimney.

"What was this place?" I asked.

"This was the sight of a school a very long time ago," Amy answered. "The creek rose so rapidly one afternoon that the school was flooded with water before most could escape."

My heart sank. Even though we had just encountered two souls of little children a few hours earlier, I still couldn't help but feel saddened. There was no back story provided to me for the first two, but now, I knew beforehand what happened to these little ones. In addition, thoughts of my two little girls were beginning to creep into my mind. The level of terror felt by these children must have been unimaginable. In my mind, I could feel the water rising and pushing against my legs. Amy's voice broke through my nightmare and shook me back to the here and now.

"As the students and the teacher huddled in the center of the school the water rose even higher," Amy continued. "It soon swept away the walls and everything inside. The teacher took the step with a few of her students, but some were so scared and confused, they didn't move. They were left behind and remain here."

As she told me the story I could see small shapes pixelating into children around the clearing. A few of the smallest were peering out from behind the chimney. An older looking girl materialized and walked over to them, reaching out with her hand for them. All of the girls wore long dresses of blue or white and some had bonnets covering their hair. Many of the boys looked as if they had just walked out of a

Huck Finn novel. Some had no shoes and tattered pants while others were dressed a bit nicer. The girls formed a small chain and, led by the oldest, walked hand and hand to meet the rest of the group in the center of the clearing. As they stood in front of us they looked eager and apprehensive at the same time. One of the youngest children was still partially hiding behind an older girl, peeking out only enough to expose her eyes as she clutched the dress of her protector in her tiny mouth. Then one of them spoke.

"We have been waiting a long time," an older boy volunteered. "But we are ready."

The first to get to me was a tiny little blonde girl in a Little House on the Prairie dress. She basically ran at me with her arms outstretched. It reminded me of my own girls when they were little and how they would rush at me and tackle me after a long day at work. I was overcome by a rush of emotion as I knelt to meet her embrace. As she reached me she smiled and looked me directly in the eye and was gone in a flash of light. I didn't even have time to recover as another little hug was quickly around my leg, this one a beautiful little boy with dark hair. His hug was punctuated with a playful punch to my midsection. Soon, he too was gone from my grasp. With each child being moved on I noticed the woods surrounding us light up. The leaves would glisten slightly for a brief second and then darkness would return.

The two oldest children, a boy and a girl, were patiently sending the children to me one at a time. They had obviously been watching over these kids for a long time and were now shepherding them to a better place where family and friends waited. The boy went last. He reached out his right hand and we enjoyed a firm handshake. I clutched his right shoulder with my left hand and he lifted his head to the sky. The light led his way and then my hand was empty.

I took it all in for a moment. The exhilaration and joy were awesome and they overtook the sadness from minutes before. And then came the wave of fatigue. I was completely spent. I wobbled for a second and then dropped to my butt, my legs flopping out in front of me. Amy attempted to grab me to no avail. I was dead weight, much too big for her to have a realistic chance at slowing my descent. So there we sat, in the middle of very dark woods, me leaning back against her. A cold sweat was now beginning to form and I was close to passing out.

"I'm sorry," she said. "That was way too much for you this soon."

"How many was that?" I asked, not even able to raise my head.

"Three back at the house and seven or eight here," she answered.

She wrapped her arms around me from behind and held me up. Even as bad as I felt, the feeling of being held up by her was somehow strangely familiar and very comforting. As I recovered I began to notice sounds first. The low constant roar in my ears began to fade and I first noticed the sound of crickets to my left, the gurgle and splash sounds of the creek behind me, an owl somewhere overhead and then the closing of a car door. Soon I heard another. We weren't alone anymore. Somewhere at the top of the path, someone had now joined us.

I gathered myself as quickly as I could. Up the hill towards the origination of the drive I could see flashlight beams moving and slashing through the inky darkness. Whoever they were they were moving quickly down the path and heading this way.

"Can you stand?" Amy asked.

"Yeah, I think so," I replied and began the process of rising to my feet. I could have used a few more of them as I was still very unsteady. I felt Amy struggling to try to hold me steady.

"Come on!" she said in frustration as I now felt her hand on the back of my head. At first I thought she had shoved my head forward but she hadn't. Suddenly I felt a jolt of adrenaline fly through my body. Whatever she had done, it helped. I was at near full strength physically.

I staggered up the path until it turned to gravel again. By this time the flashlights were only a slight bend on the trail away. There was no hiding at this point so I began to mentally prepare my story. When the first light hit me I was temporarily blinded. I raised my arm to block it.

"Hey!" I protested.

The light lowered slightly and I began to squint to regain my night vision. Within a few seconds I made out another light coming around the curve in the trail. In front of me stood two people and another was coming up right behind them.

"I told you it was the same car," a female voice said from in front of me.

By this time my ability to see had almost returned. There was enough recovery in my eyes to make out the face of a woman standing in front of me. She looked a bit pissed. The guy standing next to her held the flashlight so the beam impacted the center of my chest and I couldn't see him very well. I could see the third member of their group was almost caught up to them. Once his face entered our little impromptu meeting ring it was lit by the glow of the flashlights. I recognized him as the driver of the van from earlier in the evening. He had been the one who approached me in the driveway at the house. His look was one of amused irritation.

"Still looking into real estate opportunities I assume?" he said sarcastically.

I had no answer this time. I just shrugged my shoulders and continued to keep my eyes from looking directly into any of the lights.

"What are you really doing here?" he asked as his demeanor changed to one of a bit more anger.

I had no clue how to respond. And I really didn't understand how we would have ended up at the same place as these guys again. Amy immediately came to mind. I'm sure she had something to do with it. I made a mental note to ask her about that if given the chance later.

"Nope, actually I was doing a little fishing," I answered. "I am just heading up to the car to get some more stuff."

While this brief conversation was taking place I couldn't help but notice the woman was looking past me and not directly at me. Occasionally, she would briefly look back at me, but mostly she stared off to the left of me. Out of the corner of my eye I noticed movement from that exact spot. It was Amy and she seemed to be looking directly back at the other woman. I was completely unprepared for this and wasn't quite sure what to do. So I decided to keep talking about fishing and make my way past them.

"I need some night crawlers from the cooler, so if you will excuse me," I said as I began to look for a way around him.

"If you are fishing, why don't I see any sort of lights down there by the creek?" he quipped. "No fire, you don't even have a flashlight."

"Yeah, that is what I am going to get out of the car, so if you will excuse me, I am sure we can share the fish here," I said, moving past him and aiming my way up the trail.

I felt a hand grab my arm. The guy had reached out to stop me and tried to spin me around to face him. That was a mistake. Throughout my life, I had a tendency to overreact in situations like this, especially when feeling threatened directly.

"I don't think you are here looking for fish," he raised his voice with his actions.

I reacted. With one quick motion, I simultaneously smacked my right hand on his chest and swept my heel against the back of his leg. He went down quickly and with a thud. For a split second, I felt badly for him, and then that feeling was gone.

"Dude, what are you doing?" the other man yelled.

But I was already moving away from them and up the remainder of the path. The woman said something in a very nasty tone, but I wasn't listening at that point, jogging yes, listening no. Somewhere to my side I could hear Amy laughing under her breath. I smiled, but I wasn't ready to relax just yet.

We reached the car and I quickly jumped in. I wasn't much worried about Amy's whereabouts at this point. I knew she wasn't going to get left behind. I started the car and began to pull back onto the road. The trio was just exiting the shadows of the drive as I left the grassy roadside and accelerated away. They were all yelling at me, but it was unintelligible. I was sure they weren't cheering my driving moves or my putting whoever that guy was on his backside. But I didn't stop to find out, it was time to leave.

A few minutes into the drive the adrenaline was wearing off and I was becoming quite tired very quickly. The exhaustion wasn't as bad as it had been down by the creek just minutes before, but I was definitely feeling the wear of the events. Thankfully, I was okay to continue driving as I really didn't want to allow our new found trio of friends to catch up to us.

"Okay, that wasn't a coincidence," I began my interrogation of Amy. "Those guys didn't just happen to end up at the same two places as us on accident."

The car was dark, but I knew she was there. I could feel her behind me in that pitch black back seat.

"No, I thought we might run into them at one of those places," Amy answered from the dark.

"I didn't plan on seeing them at both places though. I thought we would be gone from the old school before they arrived, but I pushed you a little too hard, that's my fault."

"Who were they and why were they there?" I asked, further curious.

"They are a group who call themselves Paranormal Finders," she answered.

"They were there looking for the same things we were. They want to prove that ghosts exist and garner as much fame and money from that as they can."

I still couldn't see her because there were no street lights on this stretch of road and little light emanating from inside the car. But as I continued down the road, I knew she had that smarmy smirk on her face. I could feel that too.

"You mean they are ghost hunters?" I followed. "Wow, I thought that was only TV stuff."

"Yep, they go out and try to document things like that," she answered. "I have been eavesdropping on them."

Now I was smiling.

"You mean they had planned to go to those two places tonight and attempt to document ghosts and we got there first and removed the ghosts?" I said with a bit of a giggle.

"Yep, they got there and those places were empty," Amy quipped.

"Oh, that's funny," I said. "No wonder they were a bit peeved when they saw us again."

It was at this point I remembered the stare down between Amy and the other girl from the group. I was fairly certain that the other girl saw Amy but the two guys did not.

"Why did you let that girl see you?" I asked.

"You noticed that, huh?" she said sounding slightly surprised, only slightly though.

"Yeah, she hardly took her eyes off of you," I said. "Was she the only one that saw you?" I asked.

"Yes,"

"Why?"

"I didn't reveal myself to her, she could already see me,"

"Okay, how is that?" I asked.

"Because she is like you," Amy informed me. "Her name is Devon."

"Whoa, you have been eavesdropping if you know their names," I replied. "And she has the same abilities?"

"Yeah," Amy answered quickly, acting as if she wanted to change the subject.

"I thought James said there weren't many of us around anymore," I added.

I guessed Devon must be a little farther along in this process I was going through if she was using this group to assist her in locating souls in need of sending. It seemed that Amy was more than eavesdropping for locations from this group. She was flat out spying on them.

"So, are they filming when this chick sends the ghosts?" I asked.

"No, she is doing it some other time," Amy answered. "Those two guys have no idea what she can do or why she is really with them."

In my mind I drifted back to the location of the old school. I recalled the details of this girl Devon. In thinking about it, she was actually very attractive. No wonder these guys weren't questioning her motives. She seemed to have dark hair, not sure if it was black or brown because I had only seen her up close in flashlight light. She looked taller than the average woman and had a strong athletic build. I couldn't really place much of an accent on her as the words had been few to that point.

"Why aren't we working with her, too?" I asked.

"We aren't even close to being on the same team as her," Amy said seeming a bit pissed I had even asked.

"Oh, sorry," I answered. "Nothing like a little female rivalry," I added trying to lighten the direction of our conversation. It didn't seem to work.

"You have no idea what you are talking about," she said ominously.

The smarmy smirk was gone now and so was my smile. Amy's tone had been a little too foreboding to maintain a smile. I pondered further on my recollection of Devon and realized there did seem to be something about her. I couldn't quite put my finger on it, but something wasn't right. Amy knew more, she wasn't talking though. Ahead of us the road lay and there was no stopping it. It was going to keep coming and I kept driving.

"It has become a bit more complicated."
"Be mindful and wary. Evil doesn't rest."

After the incident at the old school it became obvious to me that I was in way over my head, even with Amy the ghost, or whatever she was, guiding me. It was now time to bring in someone I could lean and depend on. I needed a friend. I needed my best friend to know what was going on or this was never going to work right. It was time to tell Abby what was going on. What would she think? Will I be able to convince her initially? I didn't know, but I had to try. I really wasn't even sure how she was going to see Amy, both literally and figuratively.

Abby had already begun to notice subtle changes in my behavior, anyway. I could tell by the look she would give me when I would present her a hastily thrown together story for leaving or the tone of her voice when I would have to call her. I knew this was going to happen eventually, but I still wasn't mentally ready for any such conversation. Truthfully, I never would be, I just needed to do it.

So, how do you tell your wife and family that the spirit of a dead woman had appeared in your car and informed you that you had been chosen by God as a person of some importance. And, along with that little fact, you were rapidly developing the ability to find, see, hear and feel ghosts and send them on their merry way to the next stop in their spiritual journey. How exactly does one do that? You have to have help. That is the only way someone will believe a story like that, no matter how much they love you, they aren't going to believe you alone.

And so Amy confirmed to me I would definitely need to begin this conversation with my family and the sooner the better.

"Spirits are going to begin to seek you out now," Amy would inform me. "As you get more confident and strong, they will be able to feel you coming from a long way away and they will find you."

How will I convince Abby of what is going on? I guess I could pile Abby and the girls all in our van and then get Amy to pop in? That would be an awesome ice breaker! Probably not the most tactful though. No somehow I needed to do this and do it correctly. Living in a house with three females was nothing compared to the girl trouble I had currently, Oh how I longed for the easy days of fighting over Barbie dolls, non-stop pestering or complaints of room trespassing. But I had been an absentee family member for much of the past few weeks and it was time to take the next step in this plan.

Two days later the weekend was upon us. It had been a while since Abby and I went out on a date, so, I decided to arrange a baby sitter for the girls so we could go out to eat. My level of apprehension and nervousness was at an all-time high as I got dressed and we prepared to leave for dinner. Not even on our wedding day, or during the birth of Dani was I this pent up.

"You look really good," Abby informed me as we prepared to leave. "I'm glad you are taking care of yourself and aren't just sitting around the house with all of this free time."

"Oh yeah, I'm keeping busy for sure," I responded sarcastically.

Our destination was Proviano's, one of our favorite eating establishments in town. I hoped that a crowded restaurant would allow me the cover to reveal the truth about what was happening to me. Hopefully, Abby wouldn't feel comfortable walking out on me in an atmosphere like that. Flawed as it may have been it was the only plan I had. I put it into action.

This particular restaurant had been a fixture in our hometown for many years. Located right on the river which dissected the old downtown area, they served Italian food in a rustic old warehouse setting. We arrived at Proviano's before most of the Friday night dinner crowd. The hostess greeted us with a smile and invited us to follow her to a table. Had we waited only another hour or so, we would have been packed into the bar area with many other hungry denizens waiting for a table. The plan was working to perfection so far.

The table the hostess selected for us was on the far end of the dining room from the entrance, right against the windows which looked out onto the deck. Beyond the deck lay the river, gurgling and greenish brown, slowly making its timeless way past the much younger buildings. We each chose a seat on opposite sides of the table, allowing us a view of both the river and each other. So far so good.

Our conversation ran from topic to topic. The kids, work, job prospects and gossip were all touched on as we enjoyed our time together. I had almost completely forgotten about my real reason for us being there. I was completely caught up in our moment. Abby was doing most of the talking as I really had little to say in regards to what she thought our reality currently was. The topics weren't really important to me. I was swept up in the woman that I had fallen in love with and all of her beauty.

She had been blessed with ice blue eyes that seem to be able to pierce one's soul if the need presented itself and I was locked in on those eyes as she flittered from topic to topic. Occasionally, she would use her right hand to push her long brown bangs aside or behind one ear. She did this seamlessly as only a master of conversation coupled with self-awareness of appearance could.

Soon, our food arrived and we were completely lost in the ongoing moment of great conversation and enjoyable food. I had always vowed to try many of the varying menu items available there, but settled on my favorite every time, chicken parmesan. It was awesome every time and I knew I would be happy at the end of dinner. Abby, on the other hand, always tried something different. On this night, she chose angel hair pasta with a Havarti Alfredo sauce. Sadly for Abby, her dinner just wasn't as good as mine. Once again I was satisfied with my culinary choice.

At some point well into dinner, I noticed a man across the room. He was about one third of the way up the stairs which lead to the second floor dining room when I first caught his eyes. He had longish wavy brown hair and wore a brown sport coat over his white button up shirt. His jeans were slightly faded and his belt was the exact color of the wood handrail he leaned against. The attire he wore gave no indication of his age or the era he may have been from. He would have fit right in with all of the living currently in the restaurant. But I quickly felt he was different.

I could feel him moving across the room, getting closer to us. As Abby would shift from side to side in her chair his location would be updated to my eyes. Soon he was sitting at the end of the bar that bordered the stairs, then at the table next to us. He was always smiling. The couple at the table didn't even notice him there as they carried on with their dinner conversation. But I noticed him and I knew what was happening.

As Abby moved to pick up her water glass I realized he was no longer at the table next to us. I was relieved momentarily until I realized I could still feel him close by. I turned my attention to my left to gaze out the window and was startled to see the smiling man was now sitting in the empty chair next to me. I jumped a bit and he chuckled.

"Hey," Abby said as she waved looking in the direction of the stranger at our table.

"What?" I asked dumbly knowing I had no answer to any question she had for me while also confused at how she might be able to see what I knew was a ghost.

"There's the Glover's," she added.

I turned and realized some of our neighbors were outside on the deck and that was actually who Abby was interacting with. I was filled with relief if only temporarily.

"I need to go to the restroom," I blurted out.

"Okay," Abby answered.

As I stood I motioned with my head to the friendly stranger to follow me while also trying not to outwardly show my frustration. As I walked towards the men's room I could feel him behind me. My plan was now rapidly unraveling. I reached the small hallway that contained the restrooms and opened the men's room door with my right hand while motioning with my left for my new acquaintance to enter first. As I did this, an older woman exited the ladies room and gave me a strange look. I can't say that I blame her. She may have even thought I was beckoning for her to enter. Thankfully, she did not. Instead, she hurriedly left the area.

"What are you doing?" I demanded to know from the man as I closed and locked the door behind me.

"It's nice to meet you too," he said mockingly, still beaming.

"I'm trying to have dinner with my wife," I added.

"Sorry," he said. "I was just very happy to see you."

"I've been ready to go for a while now, but haven't had the chance until you came along," he added.

"Well why didn't you just go when you had the first chance?" I said through clinched teeth trying not to yell in frustration. After all, this guy was wrecking my plan.

"At the time, I couldn't bear to leave my wife, but she has been gone for a little while now and I am ready to join her," he admitted, his answer making me feel a bit guilty for feeling the way I did.

"This was our favorite restaurant; I come here from time to time to see if she hung around as well. I know she isn't here though. Name's Steve, Steve Cain," he said as he reached out his right hand in introduction.

As I grasped his hand he hugged me with his free arm and slapped me warmly on the back; the way old friends will do. A warm light filled the room and then suddenly I was alone, staring at the mirror. "Should I wash my hands?" I thought.

I made my way back to the table. The dining room was now very full. As I sat back down at the table my eyes met Abby's.

"My turn," she said through her last bite and stood to leave.

I had to get refocused. My plan was now off the rails and dangerously close to falling off the cliff. As I looked down at my remaining chicken parmesan, I was suddenly struck with the now familiar feeling of not being alone. I looked up and right next to me sat a woman. She was dressed like she had just walked off the set of a movie from the 1950's complete with bobby socks, poufy skirt and blonde hair curled at the ends.

"Crap!" I thought to myself while looking at the woman. My plan was now completely over the cliff and there would be no saving it.

She sat with her legs crossed at the knee with her skirt covering all but a small portion of her lower legs. She stared across the table at me like a long lost lover. This was new. I had never had a woman make me feel quite so vulnerable. Where was Amy when I needed her? "Help," echoed through my mind as the woman continued to stare.

Suddenly, she was uncrossing her legs and leaning closer to me. I noticed more details about her. Her eyes were dark green and her lips were the same color as the dark red polish on her impeccably kept fingernails. Everything about her said class, right up to when she put her hand on my knee under the corner of the table. I could feel my eyes widen to the point of nearly falling out of their sockets.

"What are you looking at?" Abby asked. She had returned from the restroom and was now leaning with both hands on the back of her chair.

"You look like you've seen a …"

"Nah, it's nothing," I said, cutting off the rest of her never more true statement.

As Abby sat back down the woman continued to look at me. But now she was even closer. The only time she took her eyes off me was to steal a look over at Abby. As Abby looked over the desert menu, the woman made her move. I turned my attention back to the woman, just in time to see her leaning towards me as if to kiss me. At the last moment, I quickly turned my head away and placed my open hand between my face and hers. Gently I wrapped my fingers around her face and with a gently push, sent her on her way; crisis averted.

"What was that?" Abby asked looking strangely at me.

"A gnat, it wouldn't leave me alone," I answered, almost truthfully.

We ordered desert, but it just didn't satisfy me. My plan had been wrecked by the appearance of two more ghosts and now I just felt defeated. My will to tell Abby everything was gone, my excitement deflated. I had no idea what to do next.

"What's wrong?" Abby asked me towards the end of our chocolate cake.

"Nothing," I lied. "Just ate too much I guess." More like bit off too much, I thought to myself.

As we left the restaurant I noticed a small brass plaque on the wall. It read simply, "Proviano's Fine Italian Eatery est. 1959."

"Great plan," I thought to myself. Next time I will need to pick a much younger building!

After the disaster that was my Friday night plan, the remainder of the weekend was relatively benign. That is except for the two ghost kids that showed up on the back deck while I was grilling Saturday night or the old man dressed in his Sunday best who helped me take the trash to the curb on Sunday for the next day's pick up. However, those two situations seemed to be becoming the norm for me now as the ghosts seemed to be coming more rapidly. Amy was right; it seemed they were finding me much quicker now. With each new appearance by a lost soul, I could also feel them approaching from a little farther out.

As Sunday night drew to a close, I found myself doing the dishes after dinner. Abby had been overseeing the arduous process of making sure the girls were getting bathed and ready for bed. After some effort, she returned from upstairs triumphant and exhausted. She sat down at the end of the bar separating the kitchen from the breakfast area resting her forehead on her crossed arms at the edge of the bar.

"Ughhh," she exclaimed. "They are exhausting sometimes."

Through the windows behind her the western sky was slowly darkening from orangey pink to deep blue. The dark silhouettes of the trees momentarily looked like ghostly shapes waiting for me to come to them. Then the wind blew and the shapes became trees again. After all of the visits over the weekend, I was very tense and every little shadow looked to me like a ghost. I was nearly finished with the dishes when Abby spoke from inside the protection of her arm cage.

"I have to tell you about a dream I had last night," she said, her voice echoing off the bar.

"What happened?" I asked innocently.

"You were driving in your car and there was some woman in the back seat," she continued. I was mildly concerned at this point.

"Was it your mom?" I jokingly asked.

"No, I didn't recognize her, but I can still see her plain as day in my mind," she said.

"It was like I was watching this on TV but the woman was talking to *me* the whole time, you know what I mean?" Abby continued.

She had my full attention now. I knew exactly what she meant because I had been there. There was no doubt in my mind, she was talking about Amy.

"Well, what did she say?" I asked apprehensively.

I was leaning down to place the last dish in the dishwasher not wanting to look up and reveal the concern on my face. I could feel the cold water running down my fingers and dropping into the open lid of the washer.

"She said she was asked to take you on a trip but the weird thing was you were the one driving," she said as she lifted her head from its resting place.

The plate slid from my hands and completed the last few inches of its journey on its own. I was now in near shock. My stomach turned in a mix of stress and fear.

Before I could gather myself enough to continue the conversation, a strange knock echoed through the lower part of the house. It was a knock at the front door. The sound seemed to echo slowly and hollowly off the oak floor, up to the ceiling and then back down again. Abby and I looked at each other.

"You expecting anybody?" we said simultaneously. In my mind, I immediately knew I should be the one to answer this knock.

"I'll get it," I said as I left the kitchen and entered the hallway that connected the dining room to the foyer. Behind me Abby sat at the bar with her chin resting on her still crossed arms. She didn't seem too concerned with our visitor. I, on the other hand, was apprehensive to continue to the door.

My heart was racing as I approached the front door. I had no idea what to expect as all of my other new visitors had never announced themselves by anything like a knock on a door. So far they had all just showed up. Perhaps this was a ghost with some manners that had not long ago been rendered useless by their predicament. Of course, it could also be a neighbor. I peeked out the side window next to the front door and saw nothing. Against everything my mind was screaming at me, I opened the door anyway. There before me stood Amy.

"You suck at communicating," Amy said seriously.

"What are you doing here?" I asked in a hushed tone as I tried to shut the door behind me.

"Who is it?" Abby called out from the kitchen.

"You have to tell her, there is no more time," Amy said as she stepped towards the door.

"I wasn't under the impression that I had a time limit for this Amy," I countered as I leaned across the doorway and grabbed the handle.

Amy looked at me as if to remind me that she really didn't need to use a door if she didn't want to. At that moment I heard the sound of walking coming through the dining room towards the foyer and the front door; Abby was coming. An instant later I felt the tug of the door being pulled from the other side and I knew Abby was right there. I let go and the door swung open. The look on Abby's face was a mix of shock and confusion. She squinted slightly as if to make sure she was really seeing what was, to her, impossible.

"You're the woman from my dream," Abby said as her eyes moved from squinting disbelief to wide eyed shock.

"Hello Abby," Amy said calmly with a genuine smile. "We need to talk." I noticed the smile was gone by the end of her statement.

The living room seemed like the best place to have this conversation, not that there really is a good room for anything like that. So there the three of us sat around the living room in different locations and mental states of denial or shock. Amy did most of the talking. Occasionally, Abby would ask a question of me or Amy, but mostly she just sat leaning forward with her elbows propped up on her knees and her chin in her hands. Amy detailed how she had been preparing me over the past few weeks and that was the reason for my absences and hurried disappearances. None of this seemed to really be resonating with Abby and she began to glaze over as Amy or I would talk.

"Abby, it was me that came to you in your dream," Amy said. "It was the best way I knew of beginning this conversation."

"I was going to try to talk to you at dinner Friday night, but I kept getting interrupted," I admitted. "Zach was supposed to talk to you about this sooner, but the weekend is over and we really are short on time," Amy said as she stood and walked toward one of the windows which faced the back yard.

"What do you mean?" I asked. "Why are we suddenly pressed for time?"

"Well, it seems there are more parties becoming involved in the whole situation," Amy answered cryptically.

"I don't understand," Abby began, but she couldn't finish her sentence.

A low vibrating hum rolled through the house. Amy backed away from the window as I stood and attempted to find the source. The source seemed to be on the back deck as the French doors began to rattle.

"It's too late now, they're here," Amy said as she backed the few steps from where she had been standing to directly between Abby and the doors. Abby stood, now looking even more confused.

"You need to go upstairs Abby," Amy said, placing her hand on the front of Abby's shoulder as if to give her a slight nudge in the right direction while never taking her eyes off the vibrating doors.

"No!" Abby responded, "I am ready to see this."

The vibrating stopped and the doors slowly began to open.

"Trust me," Amy countered. "You're not ready for this."

Discretion took over in Abby and she began to quickly walk towards the stairs which lead up to the second floor, taking several opportunities to watch the doors as they continued to slowly open. Amy slowly followed her, never turning away from the ever growing opening at the back of the house.

I could see nothing outside through the doors or windows leading to the back deck. It was as if black ink had covered all the glass, then, into the house poured the blackness. Rolling and rising, as it moved it reminded me of smoke, only thicker and alive.

"It's a wraith," Amy screamed as she followed Abby up the stairs.

"A what?" I asked, more than a bit concerned. "What do I do?"

"Fight it," Amy responded. "I'll take care of everyone else."

As I pondered in my mind how best to attack this thing billowing up in front of me, it revealed itself to me. Out of the center of the blackness a billow rolled up to a height of about seven feet and there was this thing's face. It looked like a person's head, only without any of the muscle, just skin tightly stuck to a skull. There were no eyelids and the dead looking eyes seemed to be just about to fall from their sockets. The smoky darkness then consolidated into the remainder of this human like form.

Tattered layers of dark and dingy cloth seemed to drape from its body, reminding me of a flag that had been flown too long.

I could hear Abby's frantic voice emanating from upstairs, but I could not make out what she was saying. I had a very good idea of what it was though. Inside my mind a battle began to rage. Part of me said to run, as quickly as possible up the stairs to my family in order to protect them. The other part of me said stand my ground and face this thing like a man. The latter of the two sides won the battle and I decided the best way to protect my family was to fight it right where it stood.

"It's okay," I called out to Abby. "I got this."

And then it wasn't. I don't remember the actual impact of the wraith's first blow to the side of my head but I do remember hitting the floor at an odd angle and then sliding across it, the impact with the leather sofa finally stopping me.

"It can't hurt you, it wants your family," Amy screamed down to me.

"Well that sure hurt," I yelled up to Amy as I struggled to return to a standing position. "How do I fight this thing?"

"Just like any other spirit," she answered. "Grab it and send it."

In my mind I knew this thing wasn't just like any other spirit, but I went after it again anyway. By the time I jumped on it from behind, I was getting increasingly angry. This was likely what allowed it to just throw me off its back like I was a little gnat. I landed violently on the floor. Immediately, I jumped back to my feet. It was at this moment I realized my children were now present in the hallway at the top of the stairs. They had obviously been awakened by all of the commotion and were cowering behind Abby.

Amy stood defiantly at the top of the stairs between my family and the path of this monster, her head bowed and her eyes closed. She was praying. The wraith was now beginning the ascent up the stairs and gorging itself on both my anger and the emotions flowing down the stairs from my wife and children. I realized to continue going after the wraith on my own was stupid. I needed strength and faith that I didn't possess at that moment. But I knew where to go to ask for it. Whether or not I would be granted my request was another question all together.

The prayer wasn't like any I had ever prayed before. The only words I remember hearing in my mind were "Please God." It was quick and heartfelt but seemed effective. Suddenly, a peace flowed over me. The peace of knowing my prayer had been received and my little faith rewarded. Unlike a prayer for a lottery ticket to hit or a late night drunken plea to stop the sickness, I knew this one was heard and answered. I was focused, calm and determined as I bounded up the stairs two and three at a time.

By now my children were wailing, my wife crying and Amy continuing her defiant stance. Her eyes were locked in a deadly stare with his as he stalked upward. Just as the wraith reached out to grab Amy at the top of the stairs, I caught up to him. My hand forcefully smacked the back of the wraith's neck and my fingers almost touched at the front as I yanked him backwards. Instantly on my grasping him, he began to melt into dark globs of waxy looking goo. He tumbled down the stairs and landed at the bottom with a splattering thud. I raced back down the stairs behind him.

"You may have to give him a little more attention," Amy said from up the stairs. "If he is fighting being sent, you have to give him an extra push."

When I reached him, he was trying to speak to me. The eyes were mostly gone, deflating down into their sockets. The skin barely remained on the skull as the wraith used its last bit of time to gurgle out a comment to me.

"You can't protect everyone all the time you know," he said. "Eventually we will get to someone you love."

I resisted my strong urge to stomp his melting head and instead forcefully grabbed the remainder of his face with an open hand and squeezed.

"Bye!" I responded dryly and then he was gone, rags and all. I quickly turned and ran up the stairs to assess the wellbeing of my family.

Amy turned from her post at the top of the stairs to check on Abby, Dani and Carrie. They were very upset at what had transpired before them. Abby seemed to be handling the situation the best as she was somewhat prepared for the event, somewhat anyway. She was only crying. Dani and Carrie were in near shock. They could not speak and their breathing was labored as they clung to Abby's arms. Amy knelt and placed her hands on a cheek of each quivering little girl and they instantly fell into a deep sleep.

"Thank you," Abby said wholeheartedly as she hugged both girls closer to her with all the strength she could muster.

Amy smiled reassuringly back at her. Each of them then scooped up a child and carried them into Carrie's room, gently placing them onto the soft and still warm bed. I stood in the doorway leaning against the frame and couldn't help but think about all the times I had seen them this way, sleeping and angelic. "How would they be changed by this?" I thought to myself.

Abby ran to me and embraced me with a squeeze as she laid her head to the side on my chest. Both of us were still shaking from the confrontation. We softly closed the door behind us and made our way back downstairs. As we descended, Amy assured us the girls would not remember this horrible event.

"That thing was sent here by someone," Amy said.

"What did you call it?" Abby asked, still seeming a bit in shock.

"Wraiths are the spirits of people that die with a mindset of having been wronged. All they can think about is vengeance and they don't necessarily care who they enact it on. And they can be directed, like a missile, completely blinded by their desire for revenge," Amy added.

"Someone is throwing angry dead people missiles at us?" I asked not quite understanding why we had been attacked.

"Thank God that thing couldn't fly," I stated flatly. "There is no way I could have stopped it in time."

"You have watched too many movies Zach," Amy answered

"Spirits can only move in death the way they did in life, so, unless he could fly when he was alive, he wasn't going to fly upstairs and get us." Amy's smarmy smirk had returned. It was nice to see it.

"Now, if he was a really fast runner, you would have been in definite trouble," she added with a broad smile.

"Uuugh, I need a drink," Abby mumbled as she slumped to the couch, exhausted and still shaking from the entire ordeal.

"They are no longer safe here," Amy continued in a hushed tone while gesturing towards Abby.

"So, what can we do?" I asked.

"There is a place they can go where they will be safe," Amy answered flatly as if she had expected the question. "But we need to move quickly, that wraith won't be the last of our problems."

"There are few secrets left."
"You need to protect them, then."

Two days later, we were packed up and on the move. We hadn't spoken to anyone about our leaving. I felt it would just be easier that way and Amy thought it would definitely be safer for our family and friends to just not know our precise whereabouts. Before we departed Georgia, Amy had given me detailed directions to what she called a "safe town". The drive would take us two days and require an overnight stay somewhere in between. Abby and I had informed the girls I had finally gotten a new job, which wasn't totally a lie, but it would require a move. They were up for it and the adventure that seemed to go hand and hand with it.

Just over ten hours into the drive, that overnight stay looked like it was going to occur in Odessa, Missouri. I was exhausted and my right knee ached terribly from the marathon drive we had been in the midst of. We had hoped to reach Kansas City on the first leg and even though we were just east of the city, I could go no further. Odessa would have to host us on this night.

We left the interstate and quickly selected one of the few hotels available to us. Conveniently, there was a McDonalds across the parking lot. This restaurant would have to serve as both that night's dinner location and breakfast the following morning. We were all tired and hungry so there was no quibbling about the amenities or the food choices. We exited the vehicle, stretched and exhaled in pain and relief after the long cramped drive.

This was farm country, or so it seemed. In the waning light I could make out some scattered stands of trees and flat land surrounding our location. You could literally look down the street from one end of town to the other as the roads were straight and the intersecting roads formed neat and tidy squares or rectangles.

Nearby I could hear geese clamoring and honking on a lake I could barely see. It was nestled in a lower area across the street from us and looked to be a nice place to fish potentially. In the distance, another flock was approaching and their volume increased as they drew closer to landing on the dark water. They must be on their way south and use this is a place to rest overnight I thought to myself. I could relate to their fatigue and need to stop. I pointed out the barely discernable scene to Abby and the girls. They took momentary notice and then stumbled like zombies across the parking lot towards the McDonalds, the arches beckoning and lighting their way.

After dinner we made our way back across the parking lot and checked into the hotel. The man at the desk was pleasant but distant. He came across as striving to hurriedly take care of us so he could return to whatever time wasting he was doing when we arrived. The only time he smiled was as he passed the room card across the blue counter to me. He had succeeded in getting us taken care of quickly and was genuinely happy to see us go.

Our room was on the second floor, 224. The hotel was older than it appeared and had probably been renovated recently as the faint smell of latex paint still hung in the air in many places. We reached the room and I held the door for everyone to enter. As I walked in I took a second to look over my shoulder across the balcony walkway and down to the parking lot below. In my mind I halfway expected to see something creepy following us or peering up at me. There was nothing, only a few cars and a random McDonald's food wrapper blowing across the street.

Dani and Carrie settled into their bed quickly and didn't protest once as I turned off the TV and told them it was time for bed.

"Goodnight girls," Abby gushed as she kissed each of them on their forehead.

"Love you mommy," came almost in unison from them.

"No playing, girls," I said even though I knew they were likely only a few minutes from slumber.

Abby and I had decided to go out to the balcony and enjoy the warm night childless for a little while. The muffled giggles emanating from the other side of the now closed door to our room told me the girls had, at least temporarily, ignored my request of no funny business. As we leaned on the rail the wind blew warm against our faces.

"This has got to be unusual weather for them this late in the fall," I commented as I closed my eyes and allowed the warm breeze to roll across my face. Surprisingly, the feeling reminded me of being on the beach. I opened my eyes to discover Abby staring up at me, her eyes showing both concern and confusion.

"What?" I asked.

"Are you okay with this?" she asked quizzically.

"Yeah, this isn't a bad place to stay and we will only be here for a few hours," I answered.

"No, not the hotel," she corrected me. "All of this! Everything that is going on. Amy. You. Everything!"

"Oh, yeah, I guess," I fumbled and then paused to really think about the question for the first time. "Yeah, I am. I gotta believe this is all going to be for the better. To be honest, I am kind of flattered. I guess it is nice to feel needed in a big picture sense."

"I hope you know what you are doing," Abby concluded and turned away, allowing the warm wind to blow her hair back from her face.

"What if Amy isn't what she says she is?" Abby asked after a few moments of silence.

"She is," I quickly and confidently answered. "I've seen too much over the last few weeks. Plus my gut tells me she is who she says she is."

"Yeah, I can't argue with that part of it," Abby added. "My feelings about her are the same."

Over the years, I had learned many things about Abby. One of the biggest discoveries was you don't argue with her gut. Abby could see right through anyone's attempt to be someone they weren't. No matter how well veiled their true intentions; she could figure someone out within a short span of conversation. I was truly relieved by this revelation.

The warm wind continued unabated as we propped on the rail separating us from the lot below. Occasionally, the hum of a car on the interstate behind the hotel or the commotion of the birds on the nearby lake would interrupt the normal small town sounds wafting towards us. The girls had stopped giggling and were now likely deep in sleep. As we took the scene before us in a new sense began to make itself known.

It was fleeting as first, like a mosquito buzzing in and out of my consciousness. Within a few minutes it was more constant. I knew what it was. Abby felt nothing, but I knew what this feeling meant. A spirit was approaching or emerging somewhere close by. Then I saw it. On the street in front of the McDonalds was a ghost.

The ghost appeared to be that of a young man. At first, he looked like a projection from a movie camera. He would flicker momentarily and then dash across the street. At other times, he would materialize in the same place, without the appearance of being projected, and stare longingly across the road.

I slowly rose from my reclining position on the rail to get a better look. The intense look on my face alerted Abby to the fact I was now seeing something of keen interest. My instincts began to take over and I slowly moved towards the stairs leading down to the street level.

"What is it?" Abby asked. "What are you looking at?"

I froze for a moment in panic. I had temporarily forgotten Abby now knew of my predicament and was happy when I remembered she actually knew.

"Look over towards the McDonalds parking lot," I asked of her. "Do you see anything strange?"

"No," Abby answered puzzled. "What do you see, Zach? Is it another one of those things, a wraith or whatever Amy called it?"

"No," I replied. "But it is a spirit. I am going to try to go help him."

"Please be careful," Abby called down to me as I rounded the bottom of the stairs.

Moving across the parking lot towards the location I had spied the ghost took only a moment. As I approached, the spirit became clearer. It was indeed a young male, perhaps twelve or thirteen. He wore denim overalls over a red t-shirt and didn't appear to have shoes on his feet. The hair on his head was cotton blonde and fine.

The entire time I advanced toward him he never seemed to notice. My heart was racing as I moved the last few feet and the wind I was admiring just minutes ago now seemed to actually be attempting to push me back. Just as I stopped at the spot, the replay began again and the young man flickered before me and began to take off across the street. I reached out with my hand in a quick effort to grab his arm. It worked. I felt his t-shirt under my thumb and the skin of his arm against the rest of my hand. I quickly yanked back on the spirit, just as a car flew past us on the road. It was now painfully obvious to me what had happened to the boy. He had been struck as he attempted to cross the road at some time in the past.

The surprise on the young man's face was evident as he whirled around to see who had grasped his arm. His face and eyes were alive with shock and surprise. At first, he was completely unable to speak. But within a few seconds, he managed to get out a raspy "thank you sir". That was all the time he had as he quickly burst upward in light and completely disappeared. I stood there motionless for a moment as the rapidity of the sequence of events replayed in my mind. Suddenly, the moment was pierced by a voice.

"Thank you for doing that," A woman's voice echoed across the street.

"Who's there?" I asked into the empty street.

"I'm up here," the woman replied, her voice now easier to follow.

Across the street from me I could now see a woman standing on the stairs of a rundown house. Her hands were busily wringing the upper portion of an apron tied around her waist as she descended the stairs. She looked extremely stressed and her dark hair struggled to maintain its bun. I checked to make sure no traffic approached before I made my way across the road. This road obviously had a history of taking folks and I sure didn't want to join that list, especially in front of my wife. The woman met me at the bottom of the stairs and managed a forced smile.

"Thank you," she said again. "That was my son, Robbie. He was hit by a delivery truck many years ago crossing that very street. I had sent him there to get the mail from the box. He has been repeating those last few seconds of his life for years and years now."

"Well, he's home now, ma'am," I said trying to relieve some of her pain.

As she continued to work her apron I noticed a large cut down the center of her right wrist. My noticing this, and the resulting stare, alerted her to quickly cover it. It was too late though, I knew what she had done.

"Yeah, I saw his ghost out here trying to cross the road one night about a month after he got killed," she revealed ashamedly, lowering her head. "I couldn't abide that weight anymore so I just ended everything in that back bedroom. I've been waiting on this side of the street for him all this time. But he never made it."

"I'm so sorry," I replied, my stomach turning in pain for her. "Why don't we reunite the two of you once and for all?"

With that statement the lady raised her eyes towards me. A tear rolled down each side of her weathered face.

"You think God will take me, after what I did?" she asked ashamed.

"I am sure of it," I answered her confidently.

She managed another weak smile and nodded her approval. I reached for her hands but then quickly thought better of it. Instead, I wrapped one arm around her shoulders in a side hug. This did the trick and with a flash of warm light she joined her son.

My mind moved from sadness to accomplishment. I felt good about what I had been able to do. I lifted my face towards Heaven and exhaled.

The wind now blew squarely against my back and as I lowered my head my gaze met Abby's. She still stood at the railing, one hand resting on it and the other firmly across her mouth. By the time I reached the parking lot to stand just below her the breeze had relaxed some. It remained strong enough to keep her hair from her face as she looked down upon me. Her eyes were damp with tears and she blinked heavily to control them.

"I saw the lights." Abby revealed. I knew she had and I was glad.

The night passed uneventfully. Abby and the girls slept well and hard. I did not. For me, spans of brief but deep sleep were punctuated with surreal dreams of spectral visits and ghostly knocking on our hotel door. Every time I was awakened throughout the night, I expected my opening eyes would reveal horrors standing over me.

Amy's directions from this point in the journey sent us west towards the Rocky Mountains and then north. They had been very accurate. We were climbing through the foothills of the Rocky Mountains somewhere in southeast Wyoming. The flatness of the Great Plains had rapidly turned into elevated plateaus and then ever rising hills. With each turn in the road revealing a little more height to the surrounding landscape. In the distance, the majestic and snowcapped Rockies loomed over all. This was my first live look at these towering peaks. They were much more impressive to be seen in person.

By this point in the drive however, everyone was quite tired of being in the car, stunning scenery or not. The whining protests hurled in my general direction by the girls were beginning to grate on me. I knew they had long ago grown tired of driving and likely needed a break of any type. The beautiful scenery surrounding us would placate them for a few moments at a time, but not for very long. Abby and I were completely blown away by the majestic spectacle outside of the car. All around us were seemingly endless expanses of grasses and fall wild flowers that ebbed and flowed at the whim of every breeze like waves on a body of water. Beyond this, the hills led to those tall proud peaks sporting plenty of purple grey snow cover. It was stunning.

Between the grassland and rising levels of the hills and mountains were thick strips of conifer forests. There were tall skinny pines mixed in with shorter trees with wide bases. Many of the trees resembled perfect Christmas trees which were so large they would never be able to be trimmed with the appropriate amount of ornaments.

I was attempting to watch for the markers indicated on Amy's directions while also trying to take in all of the natural beauty around us. I feared one had prevented me from seeing the other as the landmarks no longer seemed to match Amy's. My concern must have been showing on my face.

"Are we lost?" Abby asked with a smile.

"At some point I must have missed a road or a sign because, according to the map, we should be at our turn off," I informed Abby.

"Are you sure we are in the right place?" she responded.

"Yeah. I've followed the directions perfectly, there is just no road where she said it would be," I answered.

Having made this statement aloud, I fully expected the girls to pummel me with a host of protests and complaints, but none came. In fact, it had become very quiet in the seats directly behind my wife and me. I knew this to be completely out of character for Dani and Carrie. Grabbing the rear view mirror with my right hand I adjusted it so I could see what was going on. Both of the girls were shockingly fast asleep. Just behind them in the third row of seats sat Amy.

"You can't see the turn off without me," she said in a voice that seemed to echo off the windows and fly throughout the car.

"Holy cow, you scared the crap out of me," Abby said in response to the jolting arrival of our flighty friend.

"Sorry Abby," Amy answered.

"Yeah, she does that," I responded, grateful that I had become used to those surprising entrances.

"Turn around right up here and go back," Amy added. "It is only a little ways back behind us."

I quickly got the Tahoe turned around and within a minute or two at the most we were back to the point on the road at which Amy had arrived in the car. As we rounded a small curve, the road we were looking for came into view. It had not been there moments before, but now it was. I knew in my heart and mind I had not missed it; it absolutely wasn't there at the time we passed.

"That is crazy," I said as I hit the turn signal. This act made me giggle internally as I knew no one was anywhere near us on the road at that moment.

Once we turned, I could see the road continue on, rising in elevation in front of us and eventually disappearing behind another rise of the hill. The land seemed to move and change with us as we progressed up the slope, as if the road came to life and twisted in front of and behind us. As we reached the top of the broad flat hill a town stood before us. At first, all that could be seen were a few church steeples and the tops of some buildings over the thick conifer forests surrounding the town. But as we moved closer more came into visibility.

It looked typical of many American towns. There was a principal downtown area with a park in the center. Children ran and played as we drove past the central square and made a turn leading away from the center of the town. Reaching out from the center of the town were streets lined with houses of all types of architectural styles. Victorian styled homes were nestled right next to Craftsman cottages and Tudor styles. I also noticed some Frank Betz modeled homes throughout the town as those were very popular with Abby and I. The town seemed to be the perfect mix of business and family brilliantly laid out before us.

"Is this it?" came a sleepy sounding little voice from the seat directly behind me, it was Carrie. I knew instantly Amy was gone again.

We found our way through the tree lined streets to our final destination, a beautiful two story Gothic revival complete with wrap around porch. It was exactly like every house Abby and I had always dreamed of buying and fixing up or just buying already fixed up. The girls ran from the car as soon as they could get their seat belts undone. I knew they were on their way to find a room of their own as they had discussed it for several hours on the trip. I only hoped they would be civil about it. Their feet barely touched the grass as they bounded from the prison they had been locked in for so many hours into an exciting new world. Thankfully, they weren't fighting or slapping as they ran.

"Wow!" Abby said breathlessly. "How did you find this place?"

"I didn't, Amy did," I responded. "I guess along with being a ghost, she is also a real estate agent. It is beautiful."

A few of the neighbors took a moment to wave or say hello as we grabbed some of the necessities from the rear of the car. I paused for a moment to look down the street. Good sized hardwoods lined both sides of the road and their leaves were at their fall peak. The sun glistened through the red and orange foliage of Maples and Oaks as it began to set at the end of the street. The wind picked up and I caught the sweet pleasant scent of burning leaves from somewhere in the distance. The stairs leading up to the broad front porch beckoned to me so I took their offer and made my way up to the front door.

I entered the house and had just enough time to take notice of the wide beautiful hallway that lead away from me towards the kitchen and the stairway to the right leading up to the second floor. At the end of the hallway I could see Abby unpacking a box of cereal and other basic food necessities just inside the kitchen. She looked very happy. The voices of the girls drifted down the stairway as they playfully ran from room to room claiming each one as their own.

As I stood there taking in all of these warm feelings which were flowing to me I abruptly sensed I was not alone. I turned to see Amy through the window of the entry door standing just outside. I walked to the door and placed my hand on the door handle. It felt warm in my hand the way metal feels when heated by a nearby fireplace. I paused for a moment marveling at how warm and inviting this house was compared to so many I had been in recently. Snapping back to reality I quickly opened the door for Amy to enter. She walked in and stood just inside.

"Hey," she greeted me.

"Amy, this place is great," I began to share with her.

"We need to go, Amy said, interrupting me from my excitement.

She never took her eyes from me as she waited for my answer and she seemed to be somewhat rushed. My face revealed the shock of my feelings as my mouth stood open and my smile slowly melted away. I was confused.

"Now, but we just got here," I answered somewhat frustrated.

"You can't stay here any longer," she added somewhat forcefully.

"Okay, okay," I said, conceding the argument to her. I knew I couldn't win anyway.

"I know and I'm sorry, but I am not really calling the shots here, you know," Amy answered honestly, finally breaking her gaze from me and looking around the room.

"Can I have a minute?" I asked as I turned to make the walk to gather my family and say goodbye.

"Yes, a few minutes won't kill us, I guess," she replied.

In my heart, somehow I knew Abby and the girls were going to be okay with this. They seemed truly happy here and nothing I did was going to dent that. The smiles everyone had were genuine and I knelt to kiss my children. It was as if I was leaving them to play alone at an amusement park or fair. They were happily content in their new surroundings.

"Daddy, where are you going?" Carrie asked as she hugged my neck forcefully.

"Daddy has to go do some work," I answered.

"I love you," I said to Abby as I stood to embrace her. The kiss was sweet and a little longer than normal. I pulled away and noticed she too was smiling favorably while looking me in my tear filled eyes.

"I know you do and we love you," she said with a playful push on my shoulder.

The scenery seemed to flow by slowly through the first part of my trip back to the old house. I had never minded being alone before and road trips were my specialty. Many times in the past I would just jump in my car and start driving to see where the road would take me. But this was different, I just felt alone. The desire to stay at the new house with Abby and the girls was unquenchable. Several times I slowed with the intention of turning the car around and returning. It was as if a great hand was tugging at my heart to return to that beautiful place. With each passing state line, I would get a little more comfortable in my circumstances and the longing would lesson. By the time I reached Tennessee I felt much closer to my old self.

"One more state to go," I said out loud to myself as I watched the "Welcome to the Volunteer State" sign blur by me.

For the past hour I had known that Amy was in the car with me, but I didn't say anything. I decided to pull off the interstate for some much needed fast food.

"Amy, do you have a preference as to where I stop for something to eat?" I asked into the rear view mirror.

"Whatever you want," her voice answered.

"Do you want anything?" I followed up.

"No," she answered flatly.

"Do you eat?" I asked curiously.

"Depends," she said just as flatly and something inside me told me to leave it alone.

As I exited the interstate, I noticed Amy was now in the passenger seat. Her arms were crossed and she had one foot propped up against the dash. The look in her eyes seemed to be both focused and distant. As if she were concentrating on a conversation or studying a painting by one of the great masters, attempting to glean their intent from only the brushstrokes and patterns. A few minutes later, we were back on the interstate, my food in hand. I felt somewhat guilty for eating in front of her. It passed quickly.

"We aren't going to your house," Amy said as the car took us east.

"Where are we going then" I asked curiously.

"Chattanooga," she answered. "We have some recon to do."

"Recon," I said sarcastically through a medium sized bite of burger. "Are we marines now?"

"Something like that," Amy answered. "We have to take a closer look at your ghost hunter friends and that girl Devon," Amy followed. "They're in Chattanooga for the next few nights and we need to confirm some suspicions about her. I know where they will be tonight so we just need to get there first."

We still had a couple of hours before we reached Chattanooga and I could no longer hold back my curiosities. There were so many questions I had for Amy, but I didn't even know where to begin. So I decided to just blurt out the first question that came to my mind. It didn't take long.

"So, what is God like?" I asked out loud.

Amy's focused stare didn't break. Instead, she twisted her mouth to the side as she thought about her answer. She turned to face me but paused before she spoke. I could tell she wanted to tell me but was having trouble with the answer.

"I can't describe His appearance to you," she finally answered. "It is one of those things that you have to see to understand."

"Okay, I get that" I replied. "But what is He LIKE?"

"He is like you," Amy answered. "And me. And everyone else you have ever known. All of the exciting and appealing pieces of all of us come from Him. In Him you see a little bit of everyone. Does that make sense?"

"Kind of," I answered unsure of whether I had really understood what she was attempting to describe.

"He is very funny," Amy added with a laugh, obviously reminiscing. "Great sense of humor."

"And Jesus," I continued.

"I haven't spoken to him in a long time, no one has" Amy answered, her smile evaporating. "I guess he is busy."

"That is a scary thought" I added. "If He is too busy to talk to anyone then what could He be doing?"

Amy didn't answer. She only turned to look at me, never changing the intense focus on her face. A chill ran up my back. I was sorry I asked.

Just outside of Nashville, Amy had given me more information on this group of ghost hunters,

Paranormal Finders. I had never even heard of them before that night at the old school site. They were attempting to coat tail on the many popular ghost shows rampant throughout cable TV. Until recently, they had been unable to garner any attention from anyone other than a meager following on the internet. About the same time as my situation began, they added a new team member, Devon. That is what their website claimed anyway. Along with this addition they had become dramatically more successful at their ghost hunting endeavors and, not surprisingly, at luring more fans, especially men. Suddenly, they were awash with paranormal evidence and experiences, and adoring fans.

And so we drove south from Nashville into Chattanooga. Arriving from the north into Chattanooga gives one a dramatic view. The Tennessee River snakes right along next to the highway on one side while sheer rock walls line the other. It was just past this area where Amy told me to exit. A few turns later we arrived on a street containing a mix of old warehouses, turn of the century office buildings and empty overgrown lots. Some of the older buildings showed signs of being rehabbed into apartments or condos.

Here and there were a few stray lamps lit in random windows or the occasional neon beer sign but mostly the windows were dark. The dark of evening only made most of the buildings look more cold and unwelcoming. Like many other older areas in cities across the South, what had started as a reclamation project had died a sudden death as the economy dried up and the money ceased to flow. The few folks who had moved in were now neighborless and likely to be that way for a while.

We parked a few blocks away from the empty building targeted by Paranormal Finders and waited. Amy and I decided the best way to get a better look at their operation was to tag along on one of their investigations. Tag along that is, without them knowing. It would be pretty easy to monitor them inside this old building as long as we got there before they did.

The street we parked on was about two blocks from the old structure to be investigated by them on this particular night. Slightly downhill from our origination point, the building was not spectacular in appearance. In fact, other than the name of the original business inscribed high above the street into the stone face, there was nothing striking about the structure to differentiate it from its neighbors.

We entered the building from a side access door about an hour before they arrived. Once inside, I was surprised at the lack of light. Even with an abundance of windows, the place just seemed dim. In my mind I thought about the night at the restaurant with Abby and how, even at that place, there was no lack of lost souls. As I did this remembering, I detected an absence of any type of feelings. Everything just felt empty. I had lost sight of Amy a few moments earlier, but didn't really think much of it as I could still feel her somewhat close by. I knew she was likely scouting out a concealed observation point for me as she wasn't going to have a problem hiding.

The deeper I went into the building the darker it became. I had no flashlight and didn't want to call out to Amy for fear of being heard by someone else or appearing spooked by the dark. I slowed my pace and felt my way down the hall until the hallway ended with a closed door. As I opened the door it creaked loudly revealing decades of little use on the hinges. I entered, cringing at my lack of stealth.

The room was large and several stories high. There were windows at the highest point of two of the walls letting in just enough light to reveal most of the details of the room. My eyes were quickly able to adjust to the limited light. I could see a few offices along the far wall and what appeared to be two large roll up doors opposite of my location. I surmised this must have been a loading dock at one time.

I made my way across the wide floor of the former shipping and receiving area for many past businesses. The floor was covered in a thin layer of dust, old papers and the odd soft drink or beer bottle. One of these bottles announced my new location as I accidently kicked it about two thirds of the way across the span. The room smelled of old cardboard and motor oil and the air hung rather heavy as if waiting to collapse onto you. But Amy and I were still the only souls in the building.

"You are so loud," I heard Amy announce from somewhere inside the room but above the floor.

"I can't see crap," I responded.

"Would you like some light?" she asked sarcastically. Immediately the room lit up in the same light that Amy had used in the old house.

"Thanks," I responded. "Isn't someone going to be able to see that light?"

"Nah, only you and I can see it," she answered.

"Oh, cool," I responded genuinely impressed. "Where are you?"

"Look up," she answered.

I raised my head and noticed some sort of catwalk circling most of the room just under the windows. Amy was standing in the center of the walkway leaning against the rail and looking down at me.

"How do I get up there?" I asked excitedly.

"You see that office over there to your left?" Amy asked me.

"Yep," I answered.

"Go in there and then into the closet," she continued. "At the back of the closet is an access stairway."

"Okay," I said, not real happy about going back into the dark.

Once I reached the closet door I tried to open it with one hand. This didn't work. It was obvious the door had not been opened in many years. So, with two hands now on the handle and one foot against the wall I yanked the door open. The stairway was inky dark and steep. The uppermost portion was illuminated by Amy's light source so I locked my eyes on this and forced myself up the stairs.

"Did you come up that way, Amy?" I asked as I reached her vantage point high above the loading room.

"No way, there might be spiders in there," she answered matter-of-factly. I noticed her smarmy smirk had returned.

"Amy, a thought just occurred to me. Won't any ghosts know I am here and attempt to seek me out?" I asked.

"They might, but most likely they will not really notice you with the other guys running around," she answered.

"If they do just do your thing," she added.

From this spot on the catwalk you could see everything in this portion of the building and I knew this was a good place to observe without exposure. It was the same feeling that you got when playing hide and seek as a kid. You knew you had a good hiding spot by how bad you had to pee when you got concealed. But I wasn't about to tell Amy that.

"From here you can watch most of what they will try to do tonight," Amy said. "I will watch the rest of the building and try to funnel them this way," she continued. This was going to be awesome, I thought in my head.

"Game on," I said aloud. Amy was now gone.

About a half hour later our intended targets entered the old building from the front. They took a surprisingly short amount of time to begin their investigating. Almost immediately, the three of them were hooking up cameras and running extension cords to various other electronics throughout the building. They were very well-organized and quick.

Just like Amy had inferred, they seemed to be concentrating their efforts on the loading dock area. I quickly recognized all three of them as they moved about the floor below. There was no missing Devon and the two guys were the same ones that I had had my run-in with that night on the trail coming up from the old school. I smiled a bit as I recalled putting the head guy on his butt when he tried to put his hands on me.

My first two encounters with these guys had been rather hurried and I did not really take the time to notice many details about them. But here I could. The leader of the group had short dark hair that appeared to be purposefully absent of styling. He was of average build and weight and had a stern jaw as he worked.

The other man seemed reserved but approachable in his demeanor. He looked to be about four inches taller than the leader. His head was shaved very close or completely bald and his face was partially hidden by a dark scraggly goatee. He appeared to be the body type that at one time might have been very strong and muscular but had begun to sag and expand slightly from no longer exercising. All three wore black long sleeve shirts and jeans. In my mind I wondered if this was a prerequisite dress code for ghost hunting groups as they all seemed to dress this way.

Soon after they started their set up I noticed the feeling in the building had begun to change. We weren't the only souls in the building anymore. The mixture of excitement and fear had begun to energize the lost and they were emerging throughout the building.

Once the investigators had all of their gadgets up and running they began to talk about their plan of attack.

"All right guys, everything looks good on the set up, let's get started," the leader stated.

"Alex, you start out with me on the upper floors for a little while before we split up and Devon you monitor the equipment first," the leader said.

"So that guy's name is Alex," I noted to myself.

"Ethan, do you want me to go ahead and start the digital video recorders?" Devon asked.

"And the head guy's name is Ethan," I mumbled to myself.

"Yeah, go ahead," Ethan answered.

Below me on the ground floor the group had set up a folding table and had it covered with a myriad of electronics and surveillance equipment. In front of the screens sat Devon, monitoring all of the output. From my perch, I could see her face illuminated by all of the screens and noticed her eyes darting back and forth from one display to another. She was very focused. So much so I was able to get away with making small sounds when shifting my body weight without detection.

Initially, the night dragged. Periodically there would be an excited radio call from Ethan or Alex to Devon on an anomalous sound or tap or temperature variation. I tried to yawn quietly.

Then, unexpectedly I noticed a new feeling. A spirit had entered the room and was somewhere down below on the ground floor.

An instant after I noticed feeling the new spirit I saw Devon stand from her chair. She had obviously felt it too. She stood slowly, leaning forward on both hands and slowly pushing her chair away from the table with the backs of her legs. Directly below me I could just make out the form of another soul other than Devon and myself. It was walking slowly around the perimeter of the room, as if to scope the situation out. Devon only moved her head, following the entity as it slowly moved around to her left flank. As the form moved closer to the center of the wall to my right I began to be able to make out more details.

The clothing was somewhat colorless at first, and then I realized it was actually a gray-brown uniform of some sort. Immediately, the word butternut came to mind and I realized he must have been a Confederate soldier. He wore a tattered wide brimmed hat that at one time might have been a deep chocolate brown, but now just looked faded and dirty. His feet were bare and made a slight slapping sound as he moved across the dusty concrete floor. I could not see his face or any other distinguishing features because of the limited light and his wide hat, but he gave the impression of being young as he was built solidly and lean.

As he reached the point in the room where he was even with the table of electronics he paused cautiously. The shadow of an open office door provided some concealment for him as he appeared to be unsure of what Devon's intentions were. She had begun to slowly move towards him with both hands raised in front of her as if to say "don't be afraid."

"Hey there, it's okay," Devon said to the spirit.

"You can see me?" he answered in a heavy southern accent.

"Of course I can," she replied. "I'm here to help you."

As she was talking she continued to slowly move toward the young man. She reminded me of a cat sneaking up on a bird in the grass.

"What about everyone else?" the young spirit queried.

"Well if I see them I will help them too," Devon answered.

I didn't believe her as her body language seemed to look different than her words and it seemed the young spirit was skeptical as well. He began to back away from her slowly and seemed to be about to turn and run when she sprang. Devon's arms seemed to shoot out away from her body like a predator snatching its prey.

"I don't want your help lady," the spirit shrieked as Devon's hands grabbed each of his shoulders.

With one strong movement, she flung him to her left. It was as if he had become paper and was able to be tossed easily by this woman. He screamed the scream of someone in horrible pain and despair. As he flew through the air he exploded into a dark watery liquid that splattered grotesquely on the floor and then rapidly evaporated into the concrete, his screams vanishing with him. I was stunned. That process didn't look anything like what I had done to every spirit except the wraith and this soul was no wraith. Nothing felt right about what I had just witnessed. Surprisingly, Devon appeared to wince as the process concluded and shrugged her shoulders with a shudder after the soul had departed.

"Dang fool, told him not to go down there," a voice whispered from somewhere to my right along the catwalk.

"Why'd she do that?" another voice whispered.

Lying on my stomach allowed a favorable vantage point for discreetly watching the floor below, but it didn't provide much of an opportunity to move. Based on Devon's actions below I had surmised she had not heard the whispers and I had not noticed the feeling of additional souls joining us.

Her communications radio on the table began to crackle with questions from her partners and she made her way back towards the array of equipment. I viewed this bit of noise as the best opportunity to slowly sneak toward the whispers on the catwalk to my right. The crawl was slow at first and only when she was talking on her radio. But when I heard her say she had to go to the van to retrieve something the guys were asking for, I knew I had a better chance to move quickly, and not on my belly.

Once Devon was gone I stood and peered through the grainy darkness to the spot I had heard the whispers from. Based on their statements I knew they too were lost souls and had been watching the interaction below from a safe location concealed from detection.

"Hey, are you guys still over there?" I whispered loudly.

"Yep, who are you, mister?" one of them answered quietly.

"I'm a friend," I said. I carefully made my way down the walk and around the corner.

There, just before the stairway leading down to the closet lay the spirits of two young men. They were dressed nearly identically to their friend who had been dispatched by Devon only minutes before with the exception of the shoes on their feet. They both stared up at me with wide eyes. Neither of them looked to be much out of their teens, if at all. And then it hit me, these young men were definitely Confederate soldiers. They had likely fought in one of the numerous Civil War battles that took place all around Chattanooga. They were so very young and it took me a second to conceal the sadness that welled up inside me.

"Are you guys okay?" I asked, not really sure of how to begin a conversation with them.

"Not really," the older looking of the two answered. "That was our cousin."

"Kind'a hard to watch him die again," the younger one added. "But we told him not to go down there."

"He seemed kinda' drawn to that woman," the older soldier said sternly as he turned to peer back over the edge as if he hoped to see his family member still there.

"What happened to him?" the younger soldier asked. "Where'd he go?"

"I don't know," I answered him. "I really don't know."

"Are you like her, 'cus you can see us just like she could see him?" the younger soldier continued.

"No I am not like her, but I do know that I can send you on to be with your loved ones and it looks nothing like what she did" I told them.

"No offense mister, but I don't really think I want to go nowhere right now," the older soldier said as he rolled away from the edge and sat up. His face was serious and he never broke eye contact with me.

"And you and I are gonna have words if you try to touch me or my brother," he continued.

"But don't you want to leave this place, don't you want to see Heaven?" I stammered, somewhat surprised by his reaction.

"Yeah, but not without our cousin," he answered flatly.

"Let's go David," he said to the younger spirit as he stood and placed himself between me and the stairs. They both took a few steps towards the stairs and then disappeared.

I made my way slowly down the stairs in the hopes of seeing the two young soldiers again, but they were nowhere to be seen or even felt. They were gone. I wondered how Amy's night was going as I exited the closet and entered the office that lead to the loading dock area. The lights from the surveillance equipment in the center of the large loading dock room were leaking into the office through the open doorway. I slowed my pace as I reached the entryway. Placing my back against the wall I prepared to peek around the wall to see if Devon had returned.

As I moved my head around the edge of the doorframe my throat was struck by a strong force. It was a hand, and it was wrapped around my neck while simultaneously pushing me backwards. A head and body soon followed the hand into my line of sight. It was Devon and she looked a little pissed off.

"What are you doing here?" she said, tightening her grip with every word.

I was trying mightily to pull her hand away with my right hand while also attempting to slide my left hand in between my throat and her grip. This woman was exceedingly strong. I quickly realized my attempt at removing her hand from my much needed airway wasn't working. It was time to think outside the box. I brought my right knee up with as much force as I could muster for someone about to lose consciousness. It struck her stomach with enough impact to loosen her grip and I quickly twisted her right wrist into a ninety degree angle behind her back. I knew I needed to immobilize her more than she already was as she was much too strong to simply attempt to hold her in the manner I currently was. So across the room we went, until I reached the wall and pinned her between it and myself with a forceful thud.

At this point there were a thousand questions firing off in my head. I wanted to know what

she had done to the spirit of the soldier a few
moments ago. Where exactly, did she send him?
Why was he so afraid of her? Was her purpose
the same as mine? It was time to start asking
questions.

"Why did…." I began but wasn't allowed to
finish.

Devon obviously had other ideas about my
questioning her or my controlling her for that
matter, as she used the back of her head to
hammer my forehead. The impact echoed in my
head and was plenty powerful enough to knock me
backwards. I had had this feeling many times
before, long ago, at football practice. My ears
were still ringing when my rear end reached
the cold dusty concrete floor, the thick dust
providing just enough slickness to allow me to
slide for a short distance. I shook my head in
an attempt to get rid of the stars and bright
streams of light flying about in my field of
vision and preventing me from seeing.

The very next thing I felt was Devon's foot
against my chest. She shove-kicked my upper
body flat to the floor and landed hard on me
with both knees against my shoulders. In my
mind I came to the realization that I could
not fight her like a girl, she was much too
strong for that type of handling and I was
getting my ass kicked. As my sight cleared I
could see Devon leaning down over me. She had
one hand holding her long dark hair out of her
face and the other was raised in a manner that
looked like she was about to punch me. And she
was smiling. Instead of punching my completely

exposed and vulnerable face she placed her forearm across my throat and began to exert just enough pressure on my neck to begin to slowly cut off my breathing.

"This is kind of fun don't you think?" she said in a demeaning but playful voice.

"Not really," I replied in a sarcastic choking voice.

At this point I was contemplating several different options I could try to get Devon off me before I completely passed out from a lack of oxygen. In my peripheral I noticed another face. It was Amy and she was leaning down with her hands on her knees, looking at me in pity.

"How's it going?" Amy asked me with a smile in a half-hearted attempt to show some concern about my current predicament.

"She can't see me right now so she has no idea I am here, do you want some help?" Amy followed.

"Nope," I replied, answering both Amy's question and Devon's attempt to make me unconscious.

I raised my hips upward and wrapped my right leg around Devon's head and neck. With one swift motion, I brought both my leg and Devon back down to the ground. She had no way to steady herself from going backwards other than her feet and those weakly folded underneath her body with a crash. Quickly I jumped to my feet and grabbed Devon by the legs and rolled her over to her stomach. She was still somewhat shocked at her loss of control in our wrestling match and before she could react I grabbed both wrists and twisted her arms behind her back. Not wanting to take any more chances with her, I sat down on her knowing my weight would be enough to hold her in place. After a quick struggle, she realized her situation and relaxed.

"Alright, now what?" she asked, breathlessly.

"Now *you* answer some questions," I answered her. "What did you do to that soldier?" I demanded.

"I knew it," she said sounding mildly surprised. "I knew running into you twice in that one night was no coincidence, you can see them too!"

"And that girl with you that night, Ethan and Alex couldn't see her, but I could," Devon continued. "Is she the one pushing your buttons? Do you even know what she is?"

Her tone changed to one of more concern and urgency and she began to struggle again to free herself.

"I'm asking the questions Devon," I said sternly, interrupting her line of questioning. "Now answer mine." The slight extra twist I gave to her arms seemed to help her regain focus.

"I sent him to Heaven," she said. "And how do you know my name? I guess she told you, huh? Anyway, that is what I have been told to do and that is what I am doing," she added.

"Who is telling you to do that?" I followed. "Cause what you're doing doesn't even resemble what I've been doing and I've been told the same thing. The spirits I have encountered haven't tried to run from me, though!"

"Devon, you have been lied to," Amy's voice echoed through the room. "Did that look like you sent him to a good place? You aren't working for who you think you are."

"Oh, so she's here too," Devon responded to Amy's statement with mild surprise.

Suddenly the room was filled with the sense of many spirits. It was an overpowering feeling, as if many souls had entered the room at once. At first I saw nothing, but there was no doubting that something was moving closely about. And, as usual, my body was about to pay for it.

The first thing I actually saw was the pair of legs standing next to me. The legs looked to be that of a male. I turned to look up at our newest partygoer, but never saw the face. With one swift stroke, I was kicked in the ribs and propelled across the room. The only thing that stopped my motion was the wall and that only barely as the sheetrock crumbled on top of me.

I heard Devon scrambling to get up or out of the way, I could not tell which. Before I could react any further I was yanked to my feet by a pair of strong hands. Slowly, the same pair of hands raised me completely off the floor. I could hear laughing, but was too groggy to see who had me in their grasp. Then I heard his voice.

"Want to see me kill him, Dev?" the voice said.

I could feel the power of this individual, both in strength and presence. My feeble attempt to swat away his arms and hands did nothing. Just as I began to feel completely powerless a sense of serenity came over me. I began to think about the faith that Amy had shown at the top of my stairs that night when facing that horrible wraith and the strength that my own faith had given me on that very same occasion.

So I began to talk to God in my head. I was quite sure he knew of my current situation if He wanted to, but I needed to let Him know that I trusted his decisions for me. In addition, the conversation Amy and I had about free will floated through my mind and I knew in my heart that God did not choose this for me.

Suddenly, I could see. I wasn't sure if the fog in my head from hitting the wall had lifted or if the room had gotten lighter, but I could see my attacker. He was strongly built and handsome, even if I say so myself. His hair was blonde and slightly wavy and his eyes were a Crayola mix of blue and green. He looked like a surfer. He actually reminded me of Mathew McConaughey, only taller. At that very moment, Amy's voice boomed through the room.

"Put him down," Amy commanded.

No one moved. To my right I could see Devon glancing around to find the source of the voice. My handsome assailant never moved from his stance, but his eyes did. They cut from left to right as if he expected something to happen to him at any second.

"Put him down, NOW!" Amy demanded a second time, this time with more emphasis.

"But you didn't even say please," the surfer lookalike quipped.

I saw my chance to strike. With as much power as someone dangling in the air could muster I kicked him squarely between the legs. Nothing happened.

"Really?" he said to me in a surprised voice as he looked down at his crotch and then back up to me.

"Really," Amy answered him and suddenly she was standing right next to him.

She seemed larger than life as she stood defiantly staring at the menacing blonde presence holding me in the air. He dropped me and turned to face Amy.

"You know you aren't an angel, right chick?" he said with a wry smile on his face. "You can't beat me."

"You don't know what I am," Amy responded.

And with the end of her retort, she simply reached out with her hand and opened her palm to him. The muscular handsome blonde whatever he was launched across the room and through the wall that separated the access closet and the office we were in, the toes of his shoes tearing off the top portion of sheetrock from the hole in which he entered. Amy turned to look at me.

"Are you okay?" she asked.

"Yeah, I'm good," I answered. Then she turned her attention toward Devon.

"Devon, he is not what he told you he was," Amy said pointing at the hole in the wall as a few more pieces of insulation and wood fell down into the gap.

"He has warned me about things like you, he said you would be sent after me," Devon said as she boldly stood her ground.

"No, he has been lying to you for a long time, playing on your emotions, taking advantage of you," Amy followed.

I was now totally engrossed in where this conversation might go. So engrossed, that I failed to notice that Alex and Ethan had now entered the room. All of the crashing and busting up of walls had drawn them from the other side of the warehouse. They stood in the doorway, their mouths agape. Alex stepped toward Devon and put his hand out to her.

"Are you okay, Devon?" Alex asked.

Devon's demeanor changed from defiant to victim instantly as she launched into a sobbing desperate cry while falling into Alex's arms.

"Wow," I thought to myself. "How's that for acting?"

"Oh please," Amy added.

Ethan was looking at the large hole in the wall, his face crumpling inward with anger.

"What the hell is going on in here?" Ethan asked as he turned to look at me.

"And what are you doing here?" he said directly to me while pointing an angry index finger.

I never had the opportunity to answer. From the hole in the opposite wall came a low growl. Everyone turned to look at the hole. From out of the darkness of the gap in the wall a face appeared. It vaguely resembled the face of the blonde man that had gone through the wall. It was twisted and ugly and the head seemed to be larger than before. He no longer carried the boyish good looks which reminded me of Mathew McConaughey. A second later a hand and arm appeared as this thing began to climb out of the hole in the wall. Then another hand appeared, and another and another. It was as if some horribly deformed human spider monster was being birthed from the jagged opening. And it didn't look happy. Amy raised both hands toward the emerging monster. This seemed to stop its advance out of the hole, however, it wasn't done.

The bottom jaw slowly opened into an impossible size and shape for a human. As its mouth opened it twisted its head grotesquely to the right. Out of its open mouth regurgitated a blob of what looked like heat. It was translucent and shimmered like the warmth above the ground on a scorching summer day in South Georgia. The mass had been intended for Amy, however, she never moved and it moved right through her, never even fazing her. Her defiant stare remained directly on the hideous face of the creature as the mass passed.

Unfortunately, Ethan had been standing just behind Amy. He had no idea she was even there. He seemed to be unharmed at first, until his ear fell off. Then the other sagged off his head and dropped to the floor. His skin began to rapidly peel away from his face and arms and within seconds, he dropped to his knees and then fell forward, landing in a molten mass of melted skin and steaming blood.

"No!" Amy screamed as she glanced over her right shoulder.

"Ethan!" Alex screamed, lunging in a vain attempt to stop his fall. He was too late.

"Oh no," I said as I staggered backwards. I was instantly enraged and disgusted by the act this thing had perpetrated. The entity hanging from the hole in the wall seemed to instantly feed off my anger and everyone else's free flowing of emotion as he quickly turned his deformed face toward me and smiled evilly. The grin revealing a sinister row of crooked teeth stained from eons of filth.

Amy's face changed to one of determined anger. She began to walk towards the monster holding her left hand out in front of her, as if she were holding onto something. With her right hand she began to motion like she was plucking flower petals from a wildflower and throwing them over her shoulder. With each gesture, a hand and arm would come off the man-insect and fly across the room. His smile rapidly vanished as he began to writhe in pain. When there were no limbs left she crumpled her hand as if to crumple a sheet of notebook paper. The monster crushed into nothing and then was gone, screaming hideously all the way.

As horrible as it was to watch I couldn't help but think that this thing had likely done much worse than what we had just observed. He deserved what he got. Amy turned to look at me, concern covered her face. Alex knelt near where Ethan had fallen dead. He was crying softly with his left hand covering his eyes. Devon was nowhere to be seen.

The car was quiet as we drove south out of Chattanooga and back into Georgia. The only sounds were the rhythmic thump of the tires traveling over unevenly paved highway and the muffled tones of the radio, which was turned almost all the way down. Alex sat in the second row of seats, directly behind the front passenger seat. He stared blankly down at the floor. Occasionally, he would clear his throat or sniffle slightly, but he mostly sat silent and stunned.

Amy sat in the front, her arms crossed. She would periodically turn to look back at Alex as if to check on his well-being. There was no consoling via conversation by anyone in the car, however. I was unable to put any words to the feelings flying wildly about within my mind. At times I would feel responsible for the death I had just witnessed. Reality would quickly remind me I was not the cause of Ethan's death. After a few minutes, the cycle would repeat itself.

In my mind I was replaying the incidents which had occurred over the past few hours. Everything seemed to happen so fast. There was little doubt in my mind as to what Devon had been prodded to do by the demon. Amy never confirmed what the thing was, but my gut told me it was evil to the core and in my mind that made it a demon. But how had Devon been fooled so badly? And what was the real purpose of her soul sending?

The feelings of guilt lingered throughout the drive. Although, Ethan had never really done anything to me, every time we encountered each other it seemed to end badly for him. He had done nothing to merit his fate in that warehouse. And then out came the first question.

"Why didn't you just rip that guy up when you first saw him?" I asked.

"I am a lot stronger when I am angry," Amy answered. "It's an angel trait. I don't really know. I just reacted."

"Angel trait? That thing mentioned angels as well," I asked in a quiet tone while staring forward. "I thought you were a ghost?"

"Well, I'm kind of both," Amy answered.

"Huh, how can you be both?" I asked genuinely confused.

"Well, I did die, I was just never born in the sense that you would think of," she revealed.

"I'm still confused," I followed. "How could you die if you were never born?"

The next few miles were filled with a tense silence between Amy and me; a battle of hushed wills, mine urging a follow up question to solicit an answer and hers begging to move on. Just before my urge won out, she answered.

"My mother miscarried, soon after I was conceived, okay," Amy blurted out seeming a bit sad and embarrassed.

"It was no one's fault, so, God sent that special group I told you about to get me," Amy revealed.

"By special, you mean angels?" I said, beginning to fill in some of the gaps in my head.

"Yes, and that is how I became, I was a soul, with no physical connections. So God kind of grouped me with them," she said. "Sadly, it is pretty common."

"Wow," I added. "So you are an angel with a soul?" I quickly followed up.

"Something like that, I guess," Amy said.

"As a group, we were always told how powerful we were, I just never realized it, or believed it, until tonight. I've never had to do anything like that. I didn't enjoy it. We are taught that killing is always a last resort."

"But they were right; I guess the best way to describe it to you is that the movies and books you have always seen or read don't have it completely correct. Evil is powerful, but not as powerful as good. That thing had no chance against me because God is on my side and I have faith," she continued.

"You know, it's a lot easier to have faith when you have had the opportunity to see Him. We've been down here for a long time without any sort of hints, signs or anything for that matter," I countered.

"You're wrong," Amy said bluntly. "Faith by someone without seeing is a much stronger faith."

"Haven't you noticed that a lot of these spirits and souls that you've helped have said how long they have been waiting? It has been a long time since anyone with all of the right qualities has come along," Amy admitted.

I said nothing in response. Perhaps because of all of the weight that had just been added to my shoulders. I guess it was pushing down on my mouth as well. What was I going to say in response to that anyway? I knew in my heart it was true.

The car remained quiet for a while longer. I had almost forgotten about Alex. Amy and I had helped him out of the building and into the Tahoe. The van he, Ethan and Devon had arrived in was long gone. Devon had obviously taken it when she fled from the scene. Once we reached the car, Amy had gone back inside. I assumed, to take care of what was left of Ethan. Perhaps there was some sort of Heavenly cleaning crew for situations like that. I could only imagine. Once she returned, we had quickly left the area. But now Alex seemed to be stirring. I could tell from his facial expressions seen through the rearview mirror, he had been listening to the conversation between Amy and I.

"Okay, let me get this straight. You are some kind of angel hybrid and you are a person that can actually see and speak to ghosts?" Alex blurted out while pointing to Amy and me in succession. "And that thing inside the building, that was some sort of demon or evil.... whatever," he continued. "And somehow Devon is mixed up in all of this, right?"

"Pretty much," I answered looking over at Amy as she nodded in agreement.

"Okay, I can handle that. At least I seem to be on the right side," Alex added sounding legitimately relieved.

Soon, he was asleep and the car grew quiet again. Outside, the landscape was beginning to lighten with the rising of the sun. What would today hold, I thought to myself? In my mind, I knew things had changed and would continue to do so. I was fearful of how much.

"I have killed."
"You had no choice?"
"I will likely have to again."

We finally arrived back at the house. The trip seemed as if it had taken us all over Heaven and creation. Amy told Alex to go straight to his house and get whatever he felt like he needed and then return. His newfound relationship with us would make him a target and he needn't be away from us long. Alex seemed excited and scared at the same time. I think he knew he would be safer with us anyway. Amy left as well. As usual, she didn't say much about where she was heading or when she would return. I knew she wouldn't be far away though.

As the hours passed, I would switch from reading my Bible to looking out the window and then to eating junk food. We had intentionally left just a few items behind at the house as we knew I would likely have to return. Everywhere I went in the house seemed emotionally empty. I knew Alex would return soon so I mentally tried to assemble a plan to keep my mind busy. But I didn't know what to plan for. In reality, I had no idea what our next step would be.

In the silence of the empty house, I was alone with my thoughts. Abby and the girls weighed heavily on my feelings. I missed them terribly. Random memories would race through my mind. At first, they lasted only a second or two. I saw a brief glimpse of Dani's first bike wreck or a cackle by Carrie as a toddler. I closed my eyes to embrace all of the memories fully and their length grew. They also became more random. They were a nice escape from reality.

I saw the rambling creek from my childhood; surrounded by woods and offering the perfect hideaway from my parent initiated chores. I could actually smell the water's distinct aroma of clay and damp rocks and hear the sound of the leaves rustling in a warm summer breeze. Then the recollections became like brief snippets of film replaying life reviews from the past thirty-eight years.

I saw my father standing proud in a gymnasium, smiling with his hands on his hips, watching me play basketball on a team for the first time. He never heard the taunts of "spidey-legs" or "uncoordinated" instead he basked in the glory that only a father of a son knows. "Yep, that's my boy right there playing ball," I could hear him say in his head. As soon as one scene would end, another would begin.

The front door of my childhood home opened and there stood my mother. She had heard the cries resulting from my first scraped knee. She wrapped her arms around me and told me it didn't look that bad and then guided me to the bathroom to be patched back together with some Bactine and a band aid. The clearness of the spray always turned the blood from a deep intimidating red to a less terrible pink as it ran down my shin. I was always more fearful of how bad the pain of the healing attempts would be compared to that of the injury itself.

Mom had passed away about five years earlier from complications with the flu. It was sudden and shocking and no one in the family had ever really been able to deal with it properly. But there she was in my mind, taking care of me just like always. With a pat on the butt, I was racing back through that same front door, on to my next adventure or injury, whichever came first.

Abby greeted me next in the review of memories. We were lying together on the couch in her old apartment. The walls had no decorations or pictures and the room consisted of a table holding a TV and the coach we were embracing on. It was the moment of our first kiss. Even now, I was nervous. Once again, my heart raced as the reality of our lips gently touching glided through my mind. I felt the corners of my mouth curl upwards as I recalled how nice that first kiss felt. And then the memories were gone. Reality returned and I was alone again in the empty house.

A different feeling now came over me. It was a feeling I had now become familiar with. Someone, or something, with a strong presence was slowly drawing near. As the sun began to lower and the shadows began to lengthen in the late afternoon, I knew I was going to have a visitor. The feelings weren't tense or uncomfortable so I knew not to fear this encroaching spirit. I waited for the arrival; pacing and nervously looking out every window I passed by until the fading light no longer allowed it.

Outside, the air had turned warmer. Indian summer was in full effect. The wind was picking up as well, bringing moisture and allowing it to feel more like August than October. Not uncomfortable warmth, but definitely enough to get your attention and remind you that soon the seasons would change. I watched as each stiff breeze removed a few more leaves, raining them down into a shallow layer in the back yard. Maples always seemed to hold on the longest while the Dogwoods and Sweetgums sometimes didn't even need wind to let go.

Near sundown, the feelings continued to grow stronger and soon I could no longer think about anything else. I sat down on the last remaining piece of furniture in an attempt to mentally concentrate on these emotions flowing to me. As I focused, one emotion seemed to come through stronger than any other, love. I knew it wasn't a wraith.

I closed my eyes and would turn my head from side to side and up and down in an attempt to feel if any one direction felt stronger, no one spot seemed to be better. The feelings were all around me. They were so strong, stronger than any I had felt throughout this process. It now was roaring inside of me; a wave of emotions which I could not shut out. What was this? Who was this?

"Hello, Zachary," a voice broke through the tension. I looked up to see my father standing only a few feet from me. I knew it was him before I ever focused on him as he was the only person on Earth that ever called me by my full name.

"Dad, what are you doing here?" I asked, trying not to stammer as I rose nervously from my seat.

"Well, I have been walking for about two days now," he said matter-of-factly.

"What, why….why didn't you just drive?" I continued, not wanting to acknowledge the feeling in the pit of my stomach.

"Son, I think you know that I can't drive now," he answered with a smile.

"No dad, no," I said as the tears began to flow and I crumpled to the floor, landing with a thud in nearly the same spot I had finished after my very first encounter weeks ago.

I reached out for his leg in an attempt to hold something of his for comfort, but he backed away.

"Hang on son, don't grab me just yet," he said. "You know what that will do and I just want to be with you for another few minutes," he added.

"How do you know about that?" I asked through a flood of tears and feeling a little pissed that I couldn't even hug my own, now dead, father.

"Amy told me," he said.

"You've talked to Amy?" I queried him as I tried to control my heaving breaths and emotions. "I don't understand."

"Yes, I've talked to Amy," he answered with a chuckle. It was his father knows best chuckle and I would always get it from him in those I told you so moments throughout our relationship, from child to adult.

"She should be here any time," he added. And then she was.

"Zach," I heard her call to me from somewhere close. Her tone was one of concern as if she were checking on me.

"Yes Amy," I answered with as much sarcasm as I could muster.

"Are you okay?" she asked.

"Nope," I answered her, wiping away as much liquid sadness as I could.

Through my tear filled eyes I focused on my father. He was now sitting down on the seat, leaning forward with his elbows on his knees and his fingers weaving his hands together in front of him. He was looking down at me with the reassurance of a wise and understanding parent. And I was the young child attempting to gather my emotions in front of him so as not to disappoint. Amy now stood next to him, her hand on his right shoulder. I couldn't help but think how unfair that simple touch was as I would only get one last chance to do that. I stood. It was obvious that all of my emotions had given plenty of life to my father's spirit as he looked great, all things considered. Then a thought occurred to me and my feelings changed from sad to infuriated.

"Who did this to you?" I demanded as I stepped toward him. My chin continued to quiver with emotion, but now it was anger.

Dad motioned for me to calm down and then began the story. It seems that he was visited a few nights ago by several terrible souls. He wasn't sure of how many there were, he just knew they were there and he had no chance to get away.

"They wanted to know where you were, Zach, you, Abby and the girls," he said. "I knew I was dealing with something out of the ordinary but I wasn't about to tell them a thing," he continued.

His defiance was evident even now as he recounted the confrontation. His eyes moved away from mine as he relived the experience. He sat up a little taller as he remembered how he had fought their demands for information.

"When I refused to answer any more of his questions, he threw me to the floor in the kitchen. I tried to get up, but I couldn't. It felt like there were hands holding me down and I couldn't budge. Then he turned the refrigerator over on me. By the time I died, they were gone."

"Uuuuuuuaaaaaaaaahhhhh," I screamed as I turned away from Amy and my father and searched the room for something I could punch or break. All I could find was blank walls and empty floor space, so the wall took the brunt of my anger. As my rage pulsed up in me to an almost uncontrollable point I fired a right hand at a spot to the right of the fire place. Luckily, the point of impact did not have a stud behind it and my hand passed easily through the sheetrock.

"Amy, I want someone's ass," I uttered through clinched teeth as I turned back to face the two of them. "Who did this?" I demanded.

"I am quite certain this was something Devon's creepy friend put in motion just before the wraith came to visit us here," Amy answered. "It looks like he has put together a nice little team of miscreants."

"The thing at my house didn't mention any Devon," dad added. "Who is that?"

"Where can we find them? Will they come here like the first one, cause I will wait right here for all of them if I can't go find them," I said as I began to put voice to random thoughts of revenge.

"Look I'm mad too But that isn't the plan, Zach," Amy said.

"Oh really, then what is the plan, Amy, cause my dad is dead and I'm a bit pissed off about it," I said pointing my index finger at her as I took a step toward her, attempting unsuccessfully to intimidate her. Amy never budged; a look of steel resolve now etched across her face.

"Well I'm not real happy with it either, son, but…," A knock at the door prevented the completion of his sentence. Amy and I were now locked in a stare down, neither willing to budge.

"Should I get that?" my father asked in an attempt to break the tension.

"It's open, Alex," I screamed, never taking my eyes off of Amy.

The door slowly opened at first and then stopped. I took my stare from Amy as I was a bit concerned that I had not invited Alex in, but something else. A second later, there was a muffled thud on the bottom of the door followed by the continued opening of the door and in walked Alex. He had both hands full as he entered the house. I was slightly disappointed to see that it really was Alex as I was yearning for a fight.

"Thanks dude," Alex said as he closed the door with a free foot and then moved through the foyer. All the while he was peeking over the top of his full arms in an attempt not to hit or trip over anything unseen.

Alex's arrival had helped to break the tension in the house. As he reached the living room he began to place his things down on the floor. Around his neck hung a video camera and a gym bag was slung over his right shoulder. He had obviously visited a drive through on his way here as small remnants of the condiments from his cheeseburger remained on his chin and shirt and he was still holding his drink.

"Oh, hey Amy," he said with a smile as he realized there were others in the room. "Who's this?" Alex asked pleasantly, motioning towards my father with the hand holding his fast food drink cup.

"Alex, this is my father, Jack," I answered him calmly. "He died a few days ago and just stopped by for a visit."

"Nice to meet you," Alex said, motioning again with his cup hand towards my father and smiling.

Seconds later, the reality of my statement struck him. As he took a sip of his drink, his eyes widened with realization and he fumbled for his video camera. As he began to raise the camera he realized his actions. He looked sheepishly around the souls in the room, evidently embarrassed by his impulse.

"Sorry dude, habit," he stated as he lowered the camera and looked down.

"Don't worry about it," I reassured him.

"Son, we need to talk about a few things before I go," my father said.

"Okay dad," I answered.

He motioned using an after you gesture towards the kitchen and I moved into the room. Behind me the same motion was given to Amy. My mind was a complete blank as the three of us entered the kitchen. I had no idea what dad needed to tell me or how it would affect us. My only thoughts were of vengeance and pay back on Devon, or whoever had done this to my father. Amazingly, he seemed to be handling the whole death by a nasty wraith thing pretty well. Pieces of this pack of monsters had now brazenly attacked my family at home and killed my father and I knew they would need to be dealt with eventually.

My vote was for sooner and not later, but Amy was obviously bent on following direction from above and I could not argue with that. It wasn't in my nature to question God's direction anymore, even though I had made a habit of it when I was younger; times had absolutely changed.

"Son, I know Abby and the girls are okay and you don't have to worry about me anymore. The rest of our family is so distant; I don't think they will go after them. I was the only real pressure point they had against you guys and now they don't even have that. They are going to come after the two of you and you need to be ready, however you do that."

"What about your family?" I asked as I looked at Amy. "Will they come after them?"

"They already have," Amy answered coldly.

"What do you mean?" I asked. "Should we go to them and try to protect them?"

"They are all taken care of one way or another," Amy said, her eyes never lifting from their fixed spot somewhere on the floor close to my father's feet.

Her face was completely calm and absent of emotion as she looked up to my father and then over to me and then back down. Without any sort of warning, a tear appeared on the inside corner of her eye and rolled down past the corner of her mouth and to her chin. She didn't make any sort of facial expression to acknowledge the existence of the tear streaming down her cheek, instead she raised her head and eyes toward Heaven and took in a small determined breath. My father reached out to her and placed his hand on her left shoulder. The mere touch seemed to bring her back from her longing stare and she looked nervously at him and then down to the floor again, giving a quick nod of approval.

"Amy, we are in this together," I said trying to encourage the one being in the universe I thought seemed to never need to be reassured. My father looked at me and smiled.

"Zach, you are right, you guys are in this together," he said to me. "It seems that you always have been, isn't that right Amy?" he added looking at her and still smiling.

She nodded and raised her eyes to me. Her eyes seemed to have somehow changed; they were no longer filled with her normal cold determination. For the first time I could remember, they had feelings emanating from them.

"Zach, Amy is your sister," my father informed me.

I had no words. My body shuddered with shock. I was totally unprepared for that bit of information. Within seconds, however, I recognized in my heart and soul this statement to be true. The comfort and ease I had always felt around Amy could only come from a family connection. It all made eerie sense.

Everything seemed to speed up; accelerating and I could not stop it. I was still reeling from my father's last comment when he took his hand from Amy's shoulder and walked towards me. He reached out with both arms and embraced me with a strong and loving hug which I reciprocated. As he pulled back to look at me, he was smiling. I looked at Amy for some form of verification, my mouth slightly agape from the speed and shock of the whole revelation. Confirmation came in the form of a second streaming tear from her other eye and a slight smile. It was the smile of someone having had a great weight lifted from them by the arms of truth.

"Now, I need to go say hello to your mom," he stated. "Take care of each other, I love you both."

With a smile he was gone as the room lit with brilliant light. I walked over to Amy and wrapped her in an embrace deserving of a sister I had never met, but as an only child, always hoped to have. She pulled her arms up under mine and rested her head against my shoulder. I had never been this close to her and her scent reminded me of my old home.

"Dude that was awesome," Alex blurted from his vantage point just on the other side of the counter separating the kitchen and living room where he had obviously taken in the entire scene.

"Whew, I need a tissue after all that. Wow, beautiful," he continued as his voice trailed off and he moved away from us. I laughed and Amy smiled as our hug continued.

Growing up as an only child I would daydream from time to time about having a sister or brother. Many times I had wished for one or the other, depending on the situation. However, I had never really felt alone and those sensations made sense now. Amy let me know exactly how it had all timed out.

A few years before I was born, mom had become pregnant with her first child. She was to be named Amy, after a childhood friend that had been taken in a car accident. As many first pregnancies often go, she miscarried very early on in the process, about four weeks, give or take a few days. These souls are indeed very special to God. Never really having a chance to live in their bodies they are given very special status and usually very specific tasks, such as Amy's.

Amy's soul had been greeted by one of those special angels she had told me about a few weeks back. He took her in and nurtured her and taught her of things that had happened or could happen one day in the future. Thus she was welcomed into their heavenly family. He prepared her for the role she would play and she embraced the rare opportunity to one day interact with the living souls of her family.

She had watched me from the very beginning, never interfering or intervening, but allowing me to make my own decisions and mistakes. Free will was not anything that God allowed to be messed with and everyone in Heaven knew this and abided by it steadfastly. No matter what the disastrous consequences were of man's decisions, no one was allowed to persuade, period. Once the path had been set though, God eagerly approved of any little miracles for those affected by other's stupid choices.

Not long ago she was informed by this angel that the time had come to reach out to me. I had been given my little extra something which would change my life and many others and it was up to Amy to guide her little brother through it.

"What about Devon, why did she end up on the wrong side of all this?" I asked.

"Not sure, she probably had no idea what she was ultimately doing until the other night when the true face of her friend was revealed," Amy added. "Now she is the most dangerous type of foe someone can have, she is alone, scared and probably angry. And the plan she has helped to initiate can't be controlled."

"So, Devon has been going on these hunts with Ethan and me and when she would find the ghosts, she was catching them?" Alex asked trying to clarify his understanding of Devon's role.

"Not catching them, more like almost killing them," Amy responded. "She may have been told she was sending them somewhere good, but she wasn't."

"But why?" I questioned. "Why would you want to do that to a soul?"

"Less for Heaven, I guess," Amy answered. "Or more for Hell, I don't really know how that all works."

"That is pretty sad, you know," I opined. "I mean, some of these souls have been waiting a long time to get picked up from their bad decision and then someone finally comes along but craps on them. Damn!"

"But one or two souls at a time doesn't seem like bang for the buck kind of stuff," I added.

"Not really, you're right about that," Amy agreed. "She was being prepped for a larger scale event."

"Oh my gosh," Alex erupted. "Our Halloween hunt, that is what she is probably working towards. We were going to have quite a few people meet us and the place we were going would have no shortage of ghosties. Dude, we were even going to stream it on our website, but that part fell through."

"Halloween, is that tomorrow?" I asked, unsure of what day it even was.

"Yep, tomorrow," Amy responded

"Where were you guys going, Alex?" I asked.

"The Denny Building in Atlanta," Alex answered. "There are probably two dozen people that have been invited to join us there and they are already on site I'm sure."

"Why that building?" I continued.

"You don't know about the Denny Building, whoa, dude, you have to know about that place," Alex responded with obvious surprise.

"Hello, kind of new to the whole ghost scene, Alex" I answered amusedly.

The building Alex was shocked that I didn't know about turned out to be dubious indeed. Built as a hotel in the late 1930's, it was the scene of a horribly tragic fire in the 1950's where over one hundred people perished. Big building fires are always bad, but this one was exceedingly bad. Dozens perished in their rooms waiting to be rescued by ladders that where agonizingly short and many more simply jumped to their deaths out of desperation. In recollection, I knew of the fire, I just didn't put the building's name with the event at the time of my conversation with Alex.

After the fire, the structure was repaired, but never regained its stature. Later, it would be used as a convalescent home, orphanage and, eventually, a homeless shelter; plenty of opportunities for bad situations in those roles as well. Recently, before the economy went to crap, an investor had purchased the site and planned to open a museum dedicated to that portion of the city in part of the structure and redevelop the rest. But there was much more sadness related to this site even before there was a hotel erected there.

Alex enlightened us to the fact the intersection the building stood on was an important part of the defenses that encircled Atlanta during the Civil War. The battle that raged around and in the city before its eventual fall was nasty and at times disintegrated into vicious hand to hand fighting. During the first days of the battle, a large contingent of Union troops cut off the defensive works at this intersection of two major roads on the northeast side of the city. As the fighting sagged south towards the city, the Union men slowly encircled the Confederate forces entrenched near the intersection. The fighting raged until all were killed. Sadly, the end of the fight was so confusing and shrouded with smoke and haze, many Northern troops accidently shot or bayoneted their own men in an effort to exterminate the enemy.

Atlanta historians had placed the number of dead at this particular site in the two to three hundred range, but many Atlanta families had stories passed down from generation to generation of many more killed as the remains were impossible to accurately identify due to the horrific nature of all of the injuries. Up close hand to hand fighting and cannon play will give you that result. Abby's grandmother once told her that someone in their family lived through the terrible destruction of Atlanta at the time. The family tale was one of ankle deep blood, guts and bodies in trenches and earthworks around the city where the fighting was the fiercest. I pondered to myself if this location could have been the source for some of the lore of so many families, like ours, told and retold.

I had never put much thought into this piece of real estate having the history it did even though I had heard the different unrelated accounts and stories. It just wasn't important to me; but it was now. This was likely where we were going to find Devon, along with a lot of innocent bystanders, a bunch of ghosts and probably a group of wraiths on a short leash. Sounded like fun to me as I was still itching for a fight.

Later that night, Alex and I found ourselves sitting on the floor of the dining room sharing dinners out of a couple of Chick-Fil-A bags. Amy had left us earlier. I had no idea where she was going or when, exactly, she was coming back. As usual with her, we were on a need to know basis and she didn't think we needed to know anything about where she was heading to. I knew she would be back before we made our way to Atlanta the following night.

The free time gave us time to talk and do a bit of planning. I had already prepared myself for the inevitable Amy questions from Alex, but they never really came. He seemed strangely accepting of her and her existence. He actually asked more questions about Abby and the girls or my background in Atlanta. Eventually, it became my turn to ask some questions of him. I didn't want to bring up Ethan as I thought that memory was still too raw for Alex. I chose a different person.

"So, what is she like? Devon, I mean," I asked of Alex.

"Well, if you would have asked me that a day or so ago, I would have told you that she was pretty cool," Alex answered. "She's very intelligent. But she didn't flaunt it, ya' know? Kind of the quiet intellectual type. She took over our internet stuff and it really took off after that. We had people from all over take notice of us and what we were trying to do, with the ghost hunting stuff, ya' know?"

"Well she isn't hard on the eyes at all so that definitely didn't hurt you," I added.

"Yeah, you're right about that, but it was more than that with her," Alex continued. "She has a very enticing air about her as well. The more you are around her, the more you are captivated by her. I mean those are rare qualities to find combined all in one woman, beauty, intelligence and inviting personality, kind of dangerous really. She could rule the world with that combo if she wanted to."

We shared an uncomfortable chuckle with that comment as we realized how right Alex could be. We were in way too deep to take anything for granted at this point. Exhausted, we decided to try our hand at sleeping.

"If he asks, I am going to tell him."

"Okay."

Halloween morning dawned dark and stormy. Just before sunrise Alex and I had been awakened by a brilliant flash of lightning and sharp crack of thunder. Soon after came the driving rain and wind. The sound of the rain blowing sideways against the house became deafening. Perhaps the weather knew of our plans and was attempting to keep us in the house and away from our intended destination. I had been through countless thunderstorms throughout my life in this state. The ferocity of this one, and the time of year, could mean only one thing. The warm fall weather was soon to change and it was likely about to get much cooler.

I rolled out of the blanket pallet I had used for a bed and made my way over to the window. To say I felt disoriented would be an understatement as I was still very groggy from my deep sleep. My fingers divided the blinds to reveal the outside world as it was being pummeled by the torrents of water and wind. At first, there was little to see as the rain streaming down the window distorted everything into blurry blobs and running images. Soon, the wind shifted and the rain took a different angle of attack, allowing the glass to clear.

This side of the house was relatively close to a wooded area of our lot. Two cedar trees dominated the front line of the woods and I could now see them swaying to and fro in the harsh wind. I could also see two other forms there; forms I knew shouldn't be there. My eyes were now nearly recovered from the deep sleep

I was in the midst of only moments before. I blinked hard to assist with the focusing they were attempting to do. At that point, the two forms became much more clear.

Only a few feet away stood two grotesque beings staring right back at me. Their faces and upper bodies were grey and ashen in appearance. The skin and remaining muscle hung loosely from their bodies giving them the appearance of physiques which at one time were much larger. Just like the wraith that attacked us through the back door, their faces were basically bone, wrapped tightly in rotten skin with hollow eye sockets. Dark vile liquid, washed freely from their open mouths by the rain, dripped to the forest floor. My hard sleep had obviously shielded me from feeling these things as they approached.

"Oh crap," I exclaimed and recoiled slightly from the blinds.

"What is it?" Alex asked groggily as another crash of thunder sent a tremor through the house. "Is it a tornado?"

"Nope, worse," I responded, not really sure of what to do.

I pried open the blinds again to make double sure of what I was seeing. The window was obscured again. Alex made his way to the window just as I pulled the string to raise the entire set out of the way. The reason for the window being obscured was now obvious, the wraiths stood ominously before us, separated only by two thin panes.

The wraiths' gaze went from me to Alex almost simultaneously. Instantly, the looks on their disgusting faces went from eager evil to shock. I stumbled backwards slightly at the sight of something so ghastly being so close. Alex gasped loudly. Suddenly, they began to turn as if to flee. They didn't make it. In a flash they exploded into bits of rotten fluid and wraith shrapnel. I turned to look at Alex in disbelief. He stood with his hands palms out in front of him in a very defensive; please don't hurt me, posture. Alex looked down at his hands as if he had just accidently fired a gun. Behind him, I could now see Amy standing with her hands on her hips, smarmy smirk and all. It seemed I was not the only one getting stronger and I knew instantly she had been the one to dispatch the wraiths. Alex walked away, practicing his perceived powerful new hand motions.

"They were weak," Amy whispered as I walked towards her.

"They were scared of me," I answered in a hushed and overtly sarcastic tone.

"Yeah, right," Amy responded as we both watched the still heavy rain wash the remaining residue of the wraiths from the window. Outside, the sun was already beginning to shine through openings in the storm clouds.

The remainder of the day was spent resting and talking. Amy gave us some additional details about the property and this allowed us to better formulate our plan. Alex's responsibility would be the people, if we actually encountered them. They would most likely recognize him and listen to what he said to do. Amy and I would dually look for Devon and try to eliminate her gaggle of pissed off spirits.

"They are going to be much stronger than the ones that came here this morning, Zach," she emphasized. I was kind of expecting this news anyway.

Our plan was to attempt an early sneak in, like we had done in Chattanooga, and then try to pick off the wraiths in small groups if we saw them. Devon, on the other hand, was a different story. She was, after all, a human being and I couldn't really do anything to her like I could to the spirits. I was quite sure that Amy would know what to do with her, however. At least I hoped she did.

Being inconspicuous in a large and populous city like Atlanta wasn't going to be easy. Unlike Chattanooga, this building was located very near to a busy downtown portion of the city, so we couldn't just park close by and walk up to it. The main streets around the Denny Building were all heavily traveled normally, but on the afternoon of Halloween they would be crowded much earlier than normal with thousands of parents all trying to leave jobs in the city in hopes of getting home to take their children trick or treating. In Atlanta, this was a well-known date for horror of the traffic kind in a town already filled with bad traffic.

We hopped into the Tahoe to begin our hour long drive into Atlanta. A few miles down the road a question which had been begging me to ask it of Amy returned to my thoughts.

"Why did you have to be in the car for us to find that town I left my family in, Amy," I asked into the rearview mirror.

"Because that place is very hard to get into. Without some help, you wouldn't be allowed to see it," she responded cryptically.

"What does that even mean?" I responded. Alex looked at me oddly, confused by Amy's answer as well.

"I want to go back as soon as this is over," I said in a demanding tone. Amy did not answer. Instead, she stared coldly out the window in an attempt to ignore my prying.

"Can we do that?" I followed up.

"No," Amy answered, turning her head away from the window and meeting my gaze in the mirror with a stone cold one of her own.

"Why not?" I determinedly continued to dig, now even more curious as to why I wouldn't be able to see my family.

"Zach now is not the time for this conversation. We need to focus on the job at hand," she said forcefully. "Let's finalize…"

"What are you not telling me, Amy," I demanded. "I can tell you are holding back on me."

There was no answer; Amy only stared back at me through the mirror. The Tahoe lurched sideways as I slammed the brake pedal down and cars swerved to dodge us on the highway. Alex's body pitched forward and slammed to a halt, his head bobbing downward as the seatbelt reacted to the force of the stop.

"Damn it, no more secrets! I want to know what you still aren't telling me!" I screamed into the back seat.

"Pull over to the shoulder before you get Alex and you killed," Amy said calmly into the mirror.

She was right, the middle of the highway was not the place to have this conversation, but the shoulder was going to be. I pulled the vehicle over to the side of the road and attempted to calmly put it into park. Alex was still trying to shake off the scare I had put into him as I turned to look Amy in the eyes.

"Okay, everything, now," I said through clinched teeth. Amy took in a deep breath and set her gaze directly through my eyes into my soul.

"That was Heaven and you can't go back there anytime soon," Amy revealed bluntly.

Alex slowly turned his head to look at me in disbelief and then back at Amy. I sat stunned. The cars speeding by just outside continued on their paths to their destinations. In my mind I felt they should all stop, based on the news I was just given. I could not believe the rest of the world was going on with their business while I suffered through this.

"It was the only place safe enough to take them," Amy added. "They would not have been secure anywhere else. I had no choice."

"How long before I can see them again?" I asked.

"Not until the end," Amy answered.

"Can they leave when this is over?" I continued my line of questioning.

"Possibly," Amy answered, "I don't really know the answer to that for sure."

"Well, if they can't leave there, then they are basically dead," I probed.

"No, not officially," Amy stammered. "It's complicated and I am not the person with the answers to these questions."

"Okay, then who is?" I demanded.

Amy shot an obnoxious, you know the obvious answer to that question, look at me.

"Uggh, I should have stayed in the middle of the road," I pronounced.

"Hey, are UFOs really real?" Alex turned and asked Amy.

Amy only shook her head slightly and pursed her lips to answer his question.

"No? Okay. How about telling me who really killed Kennedy?" Alex continued. "What about Bigfoot?"

Amy only blinked as she glared at Alex in cold refusal to answer his questions. When it became obvious to him the answers weren't coming, he turned and faced forward, playing with the radio in an attempt to play off his shoot down by Amy. At any other time I would have joined this line of questioning and pushed Amy on giving the answers to us if she knew them. But I was still dealing with the reality of how separated from my family I now was. Other than Amy, I wasn't likely to see anyone for a while. And when I did, it would be under very different circumstances. I drove the Tahoe back onto the highway.

The remainder of the drive was mostly quiet. In my mind, I knew everything Amy had told me was true. There would have been no way to protect Abby and the girls here. I also realized why I was so drawn to the place after leaving. Why wouldn't I be? It was somewhat reassuring to know they were safe, happy and close to God, but the thought of not being able to talk to them for who knows how long was agonizing.

My thoughts went directly to Carrie's beautiful little face, always smiling. I thought of her as a toddler and the habit she had of saying "hold you" with arms outstretched and fingers beckoning when she wanted a hug. Tears filled my eyes. In my mind I saw Dani riding her bike as a younger child, completely consumed by the joy of the moment she was in. The tears spilled over onto my cheeks. Amy's touch broke the agonizing remembrance I was in. She placed her hand on my shoulder in an attempt to quell my pain.

"They are my family too, you know," she said. "None of this was easy for me either."

"Yeah, but you can see them anytime you want, I can't," I responded through one last sob before I allowed Amy's touch to completely calm me.

I was now a raging mixture of sadness and anger, mixed with a pinch of frustration and a dash of drive. It was time to end this. The fastest way to do this was to get to Atlanta and confront Devon and whatever evil might be waiting.

As we circled the blocks immediately surrounding our target it became evident our best bet would be to find an adjacent structure and make our move from there. The smaller side streets and alleyways would be a good way to gain entry into a building near the Denny. We found a smaller office building separated from the Denny by only a small garbage strewn alley. We parked the Tahoe a few blocks away in a parking garage which had an emergency stairway exit door that provided a short walk to our hoped hiding spot. Amusingly, I found myself thinking if we do the job quickly, we won't have to pay the maximum parking fee.

The button on the parking kiosk was in bad shape and it took several hard pushes to get it to spit out our ticket. Once it did, the arm blocking the entrance raised at the speed of slow. At points in its journey, it would actually slow to a temporary stop before proceeding upward with an angry metallic grind. I hoped this was not foretelling of how our evening was going to go.

Finally we were allowed to enter by the guard arm and found a spot to park on the third level right next to the stairs. If worse came to worst, being close to the stairs would be beneficial for a quick getaway, I hoped. I put the car in park and looked up to notice Amy was already standing at the short open wall looking down the street towards the Denny.

"Wow, she doesn't even use the doors," Alex said seeming slightly amused.

"Yeah, you get used to it when you are around her enough," I answered him.

I got out and made my way over to where she stood. Alex joined us at the overlook a few seconds later. The wind had increased dramatically and the temperature was already dropping. The air mass change portended by the morning storms was well underway.

It was early in the afternoon, but many people had already begun to sneak out of the office early and the streets were becoming busy. The sidewalks were also scattered with workers walking back from lunch. I could also feel a few random ghosts somewhere nearby. They could have even been any one of the people walking below us on the streets. At this point they were just too far away for me to really be sure.

"Do you feel them?" Amy asked.

"Yep," I answered.

"Feel what?" Alex asked curiously.

"This is the first time you have been around a population center this big since this all began isn't it?" Amy continued. "I hadn't thought about that."

"Feel what?" Alex said, this time a sounding bit more agitated.

"Ghosts, Alex, there are ghosts somewhere close by," I answered. Alex seemed to shrink down a bit and looked over each shoulder as if he were being watched.

"How close by?" he asked somewhat hesitantly.

"Ah, don't worry about it, Alex, this will be easy," I tried to reassure him, while simultaneously hoping he could not detect my blatant lie.

After what had happened in Chattanooga, I didn't blame Alex for being gun-shy over this whole situation we were embarking on. I was nervous as well.

"We need to go now before it gets more crowded down there," Amy said, and so we did, making our way down the stairway and out onto the street.

The walk north along the sidewalk would take about two minutes. Our proposed hiding place and the Denny sat on the opposite side of the street from our parking garage so once we crossed we would need to gain entry quickly to prevent being noticed by anyone with a vested interest in tonight's festivities, alive or otherwise.

The people passing by on foot or in their cars barely noticed Alex and me. We looked like everyone else; we just had a much different agenda planned. Amy, on the other hand, didn't have to worry about being seen by anyone other than Devon and she could be anywhere around here.

Entering the office building across the alley from the Denny was simple. We discovered a side door was luckily open and we quickly entered and found ourselves in a small landing room for stairs leading up to the other floors. The smell of cigarette smoke faintly hung in the air just inside the door. It was likely from one of the folks that worked in the lawyer's office located at the front entrance. They were currently the only tenants for the entire place. Quietly we made our way up the stairs to the second floor.

While approaching the building we had noticed the alley side of the building contained plenty of windows facing the Denny. Hopefully, this would give us a good vantage point to assess how we were going to get inside our target. We reached the second floor and found the door locked.

"Oh, that sucks," Alex said. "Do you want me to kick it in?"

"Too loud," I answered. Before I could begin to think of a new plan, I heard the click of the lock from the other side of the door. I knew instantly Amy had opened the door.

"Come on in," she said as she opened the door and peeked from behind it.

"Oh that is awesome," Alex giggled and we entered the room.

Once inside the room I noticed the windows were all covered with decades old curtains or simple dark sheets to keep out the light. The entire floor was open all the way to the exterior walls with only the support columns in the center of the building being any sort of obstacle from one end to the other. Aside from the random piece of paper or candy wrapper, there was little else in the room. I strolled as quietly as I could towards the front of the building, not wishing to alert the people in the office just below us. As I pulled aside one of the curtains I nearly choked on the dust.

"Uggh, no maid service here," I commented sarcastically while trying to cough quietly.

Outside the window I could see the courtyard of the Denny. The courtyard was surrounded by a tall stucco wall topped by handsome ironwork that terminated in sharp points, much like a spear, every few feet. The entire wall seemed to be a height of eight to ten feet. The whole layout seemed to make the hotel easy to secure and keep the unwanted out or the wanted in.

Inside the yard I could see there were people milling about and a few pop up tents set up. A quick head count put the exact number of people at twenty-three.

"Alex, come here," I said. "Do you think those are the people you guys invited to the hunt tonight?"

"Gotta be," he answered, his eyes darting from person to person attempting to identify someone he might know.

Suddenly, Alex turned from the window, placing his back on the exterior wall and inhaling worriedly.

"Devon's down there," he said with concern. "She is over at that table by the entrance doors."

I peered through the dirty window down into the courtyard and there she was. She sat at a table with paper stacked in front of her. It seemed to be some sort of registration table or check in point. This was the first time I had actually seen her in the daylight, fleeting even as it was. It was also the first time she wasn't dressed in all black. She had on a red lightweight hoodie zipped about halfway up over a red t-shirt with some white lettering I couldn't make out. Her hair was back in a ponytail and she really looked quite attractive.

As I watched her, it was hard to believe this was the person, at least, partly responsible for the death of my father and the attempted attack on my family. She looked more the part of spokes-model or TV reporter than evil doer. Devon was conversing with a couple of guys dressed in all black. Their wardrobe wasn't entirely shocking. She seemed very calm and actually laughed at something one of the two invitees said as I watched from two floors up. I was intrigued and enraged all at the same time.

"We need to get inside as soon as possible," Amy reminded Alex and me.

"Yeah, we do, any ideas?" I answered.

"There is a ladder in the room directly across the alley from us," Amy responded.

"You mean in the Denny?" I asked, somewhat confused as to how a ladder in the building across from us would be of any help.

I walked down to the window Amy was peering through to get a better idea of what she might be looking at. Alex met me at that point and the three of us stared outwardly.

Across the alley from us was a window with no curtains or shades, allowing you to see directly into the room. Inside, a ladder leaned against the far wall. The room seemed to be under some type of renovation as the walls were spotted with clean white sheetrock mud patches and there was yellow scaffolding with paint cans sitting on it parked closer to the window.

"Uh, Amy, how are we going to get over to that ladder?" I asked sarcastically.

"And what do you want to use it for?" Alex added.

"Uggh, you guys are idiots," Amy sneered at each of us like a disgusted older sister often does to a younger brother and his friends.

Alex and I smiled and giggled at each other, amused by our joint irritation of Amy. We barely noticed that she was no longer there and we were suddenly alone. About the time we realized Amy was gone, she appeared in the open window across from us in the Denny. I wasn't surprised to see her there, impressed yes, but not surprised.

"Whoa, dude, how does she do that?" Alex marveled as Amy stuck her tongue out at us in a rare, for her, show of lively emotion.

I immediately understood Amy's intentions as she slowly and quietly raised the grungy window as high as it would go. She planned to slide the ladder out of her window towards ours to create a walkway, of sorts connecting both buildings. We were far enough down the alley from the courtyard that the angle of the building would block any one from seeing our entry.

"Let's get this window open, Alex," I said as I perceived Amy's plan.

There were at least fourteen coats of paint holding the window shut as Alex and I struggled to push it up. After a firm push outward I heard a loud pop and knew we had freed the window from the resilient grip of the paint. Amy had already retrieved our impromptu bridge from the far wall and was gently sliding it across to us as we slid the bottom pane upward. The alleyway between the two buildings was only about ten feet across so it was too far to jump from window to window, but not too far to connect the two with the extension ladder.

Alex went out the window first. The ladder gave a slight aluminum scraping on concrete sound as he slowly stood from his kneeling position. Slowly and cautiously he made his way across the divide, stepping only on the rungs of the ladder. It took less than thirty seconds for his entire journey. As he reached the other side he calmly lowered himself back down to a crouch and squeezed his way through the open Denny side window. His head banged solidly on the bottom of the window as he entered the room and his cursing had to be muffled by Amy's hand clasped across his mouth. Even though his voice was muffled, I could still make out the different swear words.

I waited for Amy to reappear in the window before I began my trip across the alley. She returned, this time with her now so familiar smarmy smirk, obviously enjoying the entirety of the situation, and I began to move out the window. As I walked across the ladder I took a second to look up at the Denny building now looming above me. At first there was nothing spectacular about the view, but then I noticed something strange.

Almost all of the windows of the twelve floors above us were not covered or blocked in any way, but just inside many of them there seemed to be shadows. They were the shapes and forms of human outlines but they weren't moving, they were standing very still. There were no faces or arms or hands, only the dark unmoving outlines of people that seemed to be looking out at us. A strange chill ran through my body and I felt a little sick to my stomach. This hastened my crossing and I quickly dropped down and entered the room taking care not to smack my head the way Alex had.

"I think we are busted, there are people in almost every window looking out at us," I divulged.

"What, are you sure?" Alex answered.

"I don't think so," Amy countered. She seemed pretty sure of herself and it gave me pause to second guess what my eyes had just seen.

"What else could it have been?" I replied.

"I don't hear anyone on the floor above us," Alex said as he moved toward the door.

"Guys, calm down, there isn't a soul in this building right now other than us," Amy said reassuringly.

I knew they weren't ghosts as I felt no such presence when I entered the room so I began to relax just a bit. Alex opened the door that lead into the hallway and peaked out. After a quick glance around, he slowly closed the door.

"Nothing going on out there, I think we're okay," he said with a genuine sound of relief in his voice.

"That was creepy, almost every window up there looked like it had a figure standing in it. I don't know what it was but it made me feel uneasy at best," I exclaimed as I tried to reason with what I had seen.

Alex had informed us earlier of their team's plans for the ghost hunt on that night. Ethan, Alex and Devon would each lead a team of three to four guests on a hunt through different parts of the Denny building. Once each team had completed their hunt, they would all meet back up on the top floor for some food and drinks, and to recap the night's events. We were unsure of how Devon planned on keeping with this plan seeing how Ethan and Alex weren't present in the capacities that had been originally planned. What was obvious was Devon definitely had something planned for all these folks and it likely wasn't going to be much fun for them.

We had discussed the need to get Devon by herself in an attempt to neutralize her, but we had yet to figure out how exactly this was to be done. Suddenly, Alex's face seemed to light up with realization. He reminded me of a little kid that had just gotten a great idea or realized he needed to go to the bathroom. A quick wave of his hands in excitement appeared to allow this thought to be articulated.

"Wait a minute, if I know Devon, she will make a final trip around the premises to do one last check on everything," Alex spilled out his thoughts with exhilaration. "She is kind of anal that way. I can just about guarantee she will make her way to the top to double check things there."

"We just need to get up there before her," Amy concluded.

"Are you sure?" I questioned him.

"Oh yeah bro, Ethan and I are terrible at details so we turned over that picking fly poop out of pepper stuff to her, she'll double check everything," he answered, beaming and nodding with confidence.

"We need to get going then, because here comes nightfall," Amy said as she peered out the window looking up and down the alley below. "Zach, help me get the ladder back in."

The hallway was dark and getting darker. The little light the window at the far end of the hall allowed in was rapidly disappearing as the sun lowered itself. We cautiously made our way down the narrow passage towards the window. As we moved closer to that end of the building, I noticed that most of the doors along the hall were open. This had not been the case around the room we entered the building through.

We slowed as we reached the first opening. I was in the lead and so I took it upon myself to stop Alex and Amy and quietly peek into the open room, as we didn't need any surprises at this point of our little operation. To this point, I had not really felt many nerves, but as I slowly pushed my head around the door frame I was nervous. At first, I didn't really notice anything strange. But as my vision adapted, I was startled to notice a figure standing just to the right of the window. I quickly pulled my head back to prevent being noticed and motioned for Alex and Amy to move back down the hall a few feet.

"There is someone in that room, standing by the window," I revealed in a whisper that any of my grade school teachers would have been proud of.

"There is no way," Amy answered in a not so hushed whisper.

"I told you I saw people standing in the windows," I protested a bit louder than my first.

"Dude, Devon must have look-outs posted for us," Alex added.

"Let me go look," Amy said sounding a little perturbed.

"Alex, even if it is a person we can handle them, don't sweat this," I whispered to Alex.

Amy quietly walked down the hall and stood defiantly in the doorway. I was impressed and concerned all at the same time until I remembered the only people that could see her were people Amy chose. She disappeared through the doorway and Alex and I waited for any sounds or signs of trouble, none came. After a few tense seconds, Amy re-entered the hallway and made her way back to us.

"Who's in there?" Alex asked.

"No one, it's a mannequin," Amy answered matter-of-factly.

"A mannequin?" I retorted. "What is a mannequin doing up here?"

"I don't know. It's dressed in period clothing, like from the 1920's or 30's," Amy continued.

"Weird," I responded.

"We need to keep going," Amy said. "It is almost dark."

We continued down the hall and within a few
seconds discovered another figure standing near
the window within an open room. I cautiously
entered the room. Amy followed and Alex stood
just outside in the hall. I needed to see if
this was also a dummy. As I got closer, I could
make out what seemed to be a uniform being
worn by the mannequin. This uniform was light
in color; however, it had become too dark to
really make out any details.

"Amy, can you light us up?" I asked.

Immediately there was a warm light surrounding
us and within the room it became much easier to
see. There was no furniture; no drapes on the
windows and the walls were completely empty. The
only thing within the room was this mannequin.
It was obviously a male and the uniform was now
obviously evident.

"This guy is dressed in a Confederate uniform,"
I said as Amy moved past me to the other side
of the window.

From there, she had a much better view of the
dummy dressed in Civil War era garb. It stood
saliently, peering out the window, standing his
post. I moved around from behind it to get a
better look. The face was weathered and looked
old. The eyes reminded me of a shark's, they
were black and lifeless. Oddly, the mannequin
had hair. As I looked over it, I noticed that it
even seemed to have hair on its hands and arms.

"This thing looks old," I said. "Almost like
an antique or something."

"It doesn't look pleasant to me at all," Amy
revealed.

"Dude, what's up with the mannequins?" Alex wondered aloud.

"Good question," I responded. "It's almost like they are museum pieces or something."

"Strange," Amy added as she looked closer at the face of the rebel soldier mannequin. She almost seemed to be looking into this thing's soul, if it had one.

"Maybe these were going to be part of the exhibits here," I pondered outwardly, "but why are they at the windows."

At that moment, I picked up on a new sense within the room. It was very faint and not steady, but it was there. Somewhere, not far from us, was a spirit of some sort.

"I feel a ghost or spirit," I revealed.

"It's starting, we need to get to the stairs and get up to the top," Amy answered hurriedly.

As we left the room I caught another sensation, a smell. It was the very faint smell of death. Before I could react to it, it was gone. Amy exited and I followed. Knowing we were now short on time, we didn't stop to investigate any of the other rooms as we made our way down the hall. But peering in the open doors as we quickly passed revealed many more rooms with a mannequin posted at the window. All seemed to be dressed in early twentieth century clothing or as Civil War soldiers. Occasionally, there would appear a girl figure, or a child, but most were males, all were eerie.

The end of the hall revealed one last open door. This doorway led directly into the stairwell we sought. We quickly began to ascend the stairs. With each step I realized there was no way to traverse them quietly. Almost all gave some level of creak or pop, perfect for revealing our location to anyone on either floor above or below us.

By the time we were several floors up, my mind was racing forward to the future and what our next steps should be.

"Which floor should we get off on?" I asked Alex.

"Not sure, should be one of the top two," Alex answered through heavy breaths. The stairs were obviously taking their toll on him by this point.

Amy was far ahead and I noticed she barely made a sound on each successive creaky stair tread. This was reassuring as I definitely didn't want to announce our approach to anyone that might be waiting above. By the time we made the turn on the last approach to the second highest floor, Alex was moving much slower. I could see that he was somewhat embarrassed by his lack of conditioning.

"Man, I used to be able to do stairs all day long," Alex said panting.

"C'mon dude, they're coming up the stairs behind us," I lied to him in the hopes of getting him to move a bit faster.

"What?" Alex said with concern as he looked over his shoulder and picked up the pace.

The open door to the next floor revealed an ominous sight. As we entered, the light Amy was emanating for us illuminated the details. This was obviously a ball room of some sort at one time. The space was wide open and revealed a beautifully adorned ceiling covered with magnificent paintings bordered by opulent trim and moldings. The floor was solid wood plank, probably pine, depending on when it was put down and the sheen of the finish gave extra depth to the room.

Distributed all around the ballroom were more of those creepy mannequins. Gathered in groups of three to four, there looked to be somewhere between twelve and fifteen figures scattered around the perimeter. In the center, of the open space were two additional mannequins. One was another soldier, but this one seemed to be more sharply dressed, as if he were some sort of officer. Standing next to him was the figure of a fireman. However, this firefighter seemed to be missing a limb. In my mind, I found myself wondering if this was done for effect or if this thing really was just missing an arm.

Amy proceeded deeper into the ballroom and Alex and I followed. Her light cast strange shadows across the faces of the mannequins. At times their faces and mouths appeared to be moving, as if they were conversing about the three of us now intruding on their space. The entire scene was unsettling.

My eyes moved over the groupings of dummies and I was drawn to the strange pairing of an adolescent boy, a soldier and an older looking man dressed plainly. As I walked their faces continued to seem to move in conversation. I immediately felt paranoid as I felt they could easily be talking about me. The boy mannequin was dressed in tattered clothes and had no shoes on his feet. Of the three, his face bothered me the most. It appeared dirty and impressed on me that he could have been thinking about different ways to separate my head from my body.

"Man, these things are ridiculous," I finally said in a vain attempt to lower the obviously skyrocketing level of unease in the room.

"They are here for a reason," Amy added. "I just don't know what, but I fear we will soon."

"I sure would like to take a few of these out," Alex added.

"Too noisy, but I concur," I replied.

As I approached the trio I was fixated on, an overwhelming sensation rolled over me. It felt similar to a wave of nausea, originating in my stomach and radiating down both thighs. I stopped to react and found myself bending at the waist in an effort to combat the sick feeling now racking my body. Amy noticed first.

"What's wrong?" she said worriedly.

"Don't know, I just feel terrible all of a sudden," I answered.

And then I knew what was happening. The sensations became the same as the night the wraith came to our house, only much more. It was as if there were multiple evil spirits rapidly approaching from different directions, their presence, until now, somehow masked. It was a trap, and we had walked right into it.

"Oh crap, we have to get to out of here," I blurted out.

"Why, what's going on?" Alex said as he backed his way to where Amy and I stood.

"Is it the wraiths, are they coming?" Amy asked.

"Nope, they're already here," I answered.

The trio of mannequins closest to us was now definitely moving. Slowly at first as if they were filling up with fuel, they began to come to life. The older plain clothed figure turned first. As he turned, the right side of his body burst into flame. Within seconds the fire was gone and he was now a grotesque smoldering burn victim. And he looked pissed.

The boy moved next. He stepped forward, out of the shadow cast by the soldier, and revealed a demonic face, swollen and battered as if beaten severely. He seemed to be the farthest along in this transformation process all of the mannequins were now going through as he moved towards us at a slow but steady pace.

The soldier wasn't moving towards us. Instead, he appeared to be moving around us, in an effort to cut us off from any escape attempt. Amy turned to keep him in her sight and was very nearly face to face with him.

"Ma'am," the soldier said politely in a growling ancient voice as he tipped his hat. "We were told we might have some visitors."

"Oh yeah, we know who you are," the boy said in an evil voice that matched his brutalized appearance. "We gonna kill you."

"Ahh, the mannequins are talking, dang it" Alex said in a whine.

"You're quick, ain't cha'," the burned man responded as he moved to complete the triangle entrapment they were attempting to place.

"And your ugly," Alex responded to his taunt. "I bet your mom is too."

"My mom's been dead for a long time boy, you think I care?" the burn victim retorted.

The other mannequins were also beginning to move towards us; albeit slowly so I knew we still had time to fight our way out of this room. In my mind, I knew the stairway was our best bet. The nauseas feeling was now gone. It had been replaced by a surge of fearful anger. An emotion I had come to know as quite useful in situations like this one. I thought back to the first ghost encounter in my living room and then my mind moved quickly on to the beat down of the wraith on the stairs.

It was all very clear now to me, this plan I needed to follow. I bowed my head and gathered my thoughts into one singular stream of prayer and praise. Amy was now in the same position, doing the exact same thing, I assumed.

"What are you guys doing?" Alex screamed as he smacked Amy and I each with one of his hands.

"Ther're prayin', dumbass," said the soldier in a mocking taunt of Alex. "Probably wouldn't hurt you to do the same, boy."

My eyes opened and I saw the old soldier was now practically in Alex's face, but Alex stood his ground. He may have been scared, but he wasn't one to back down from a threat, even from a long dead individual that, in life, had made a living on killing. But I knew Alex couldn't handle this fight, so I intervened.

The soldier wasn't looking directly at me, but he had made the mistake of being the spirit closest to me. I tapped him on his shoulder knowing that simple touch would most likely not rid us of him as he was here to fight. It had been his nature for a long time now.

His face turned to acknowledge my tap and when he did I kicked his knee inward with as much force as I could manage. With a loud pop, he crashed to the floor, his knee displaced and his leg now unusable.

"You may be a big nasty evil spirit, but you are still bound by the limitations of that body," I said with a serious but sarcastic tone.

The old soldier still had plenty of fight left in him as he swung wildly with a right fist as he fell. I had to duck to prevent being nailed. This gave the boy time to come after me with fists and fingernails flying. He landed two hard blows to my ribs and began to tear at my clothes with his long disgusting nails. I began to back up in an attempt to defend myself. As I did this I caught a glimpse of Amy dashing away from me and towards the burned man who was moving towards her, arms outstretched in a threatening manner.

Thanks to my quick shot to the knee of the soldier, it was now two on two and Amy was quickly dispatching the burned man with a series of blocked punches and devastating slaps. Unfortunately for the burn victim, her slaps carried much more power than a typical girl slap. With each impact of her open hand, he lost more and more flesh until soon there was nothing left of his head and neck. He stood no chance against this angel-human soul hybrid with an attitude.

All that was left was to remove the threat of the young boy and we could make our way out of the room. He was continuing to attack me as I wrestled with his arms. Quickly I had control of both of his limbs, but he had more to fight with and I found this out the hard way with a resounding bite to my forearm. That pissed me off. Without any regard for anyone else standing around me, I wildly scooped up the boy and body slammed him on the floor right in front of Alex.

"Time for you to leave," I said as I placed my right forearm across his neck and grasped his hair with my free hand. This was more than enough touching to send this deprived soul to a different place.

"Let's go," Amy screamed as she grabbed my arm and lifted me to my feet.

Alex was already almost to the stairway door as Amy and I sprinted to catch up. Behind us the soldier continued to crawl towards us and the remainder of the mannequins were now fully alive and following. Once inside the stairwell, we realized there was movement and sound on the stairs below us.

"Go up," I said. I placed my hand squarely on Alex's lower back and began to push him up the stairs. We were only one floor from the top and it was obvious we couldn't go down, so, up it had to be.

We reached the door to the top floor and I shoved it open with a mighty push on the bar.

Once inside, Alex quickly closed the door and leaned against it.

"Dude, what the fff...," Alex began. He was stopped by Amy's calming index finger across his lips.

"Shhhhh, don't say that word," Amy said softly but sternly. "Yes Alex, all of the mannequins are filled with evil spirits and they are coming to life and trying to kill us, okay. Now stay calm." I couldn't help but smile and laugh inwardly at the understatement of the century from Amy. Alex was speechless.

"So, it has started," a voice echoed through the room.

I turned, but saw nothing. The room was very dark and even Amy's luminescence didn't seem to ease the blackness. The voice had come from behind us at a relatively close distance. Amy stepped forward and I raised my hands to defend myself from whatever might be about to come out of the darkness.

There was a click and suddenly light filled the space. There before us stood Devon with a large flashlight.

"Devon?" Alex asked inquisitively.

"Hey Alex," Devon confirmed.

"You can't get away," Devon revealed. "There are too many of them and they are all on a mission."

"What about you?" Amy responded. "You don't really think you are going to be able to control this situation, do you?"

"I will be fine. You see Jeff, the angel you killed in Chattanooga; he set all of this up. He locked all of the spirits in those mannequins; they were just waiting for the right time to come out," Devon revealed.

"Angels don't work with wraiths, Devon," Amy responded angrily. "That is what is in those mannequins. Not regular old spirits but wraiths. And that thing wasn't an angel; he lied to you and deceived you and now look at all the damage you have done."

"How would you know?" Devon retorted calmly. "Did you ask him before you pulled him apart like a bug?"

"He *was* a freakin' bug," I chimed in. "Can't you see what is going on; you're on the wrong side here."

"And these things are going to turn on you," Amy added as the door received a blow from the other side.

"Oh crap!" Alex chirped and leaned a little harder into the door. "There's no lock on this thing, guys, and I can't hold it forever."

"What about all of the people you brought here tonight, Devon?" I asked. "What do you think those little pets of yours are going to do to them?"

Another bang on the door brought a voice with it.

"Devon, are you in there?" a male's voice asked from the other side.

"That doesn't feel like a spirit, it's gotta be a person, Amy," I said as I realized one of the invitees had made his way up the stairs and was now dangerously standing between us and our pursuers. "We have to let him in."

Alex opened the door and a young man in his late twenties appeared in the glow of Devon's flashlight. He had dark clothing on and his wavy brown hair seemed to blend with the darkness of the stairwell.

"You okay?" the young man asked, looking at Devon.

Devon never had a chance to answer. From behind the young man, a large boney hand reached down out of the dark and grasped his chin, pulling it violently upward, nearly tearing his head from his frame. His now lifeless body slumped to the floor and was quickly slid out of the way by a wraith which appeared to be dressed in the manner of our other soldier friends.

The wraith was quite large even though there didn't appear to be a lot of muscle on his frame. He now blocked the entire doorway and behind him more were coming up the stairs. There was no expression on his face. He only glared at each of us in a robotic manner as if he couldn't quite decide who would be his next kill. Amy lurched forward with a kick to its midsection. The blow did little, but did manage to move the evil spirit back just enough to allow the door to be shut again. Alex saw this opportunity and quickly shut the door and slammed his back against it.

"This isn't going to keep him out long, guys," Alex said with urgency.

Devon had not moved. She stood in the exact same spot with her mouth hanging open. Her eyes revealed a deep sense of shock and betrayal and she seemed to be trying to put words to her thoughts, to no avail. Shockingly, she moved toward the door.

"I don't understand," she mumbled. "They weren't supposed to touch anyone. They are here to protect the souls from you guys while I move them on to a better place."

Amy stepped in front of her, blocking her zombie like walk to the door. Behind her, Alex was leaning on the door as hard as he could. I ran over to help him, never taking Devon from my sight.

"I can fix this," Devon said as she tried to move Amy to the side.

"No, Devon, you can't," Amy responded. "It is done now and nothing you say or do will change that fact."

The force being exerted on the door was getting heavier. At times it would open an inch or two and Alex and I were able to force it back closed. I could hear mumbling just on the other side. It was a disturbing low muttering as if multiple languages were being spoken in a low hushed tone. The feelings were many now and I knew that more and more wraiths were ascending the stairs to assault us, there was no mistaking that.

"Let me try," Devon pleaded. "Remember, I can send these things just like he can."

"Devon, no," Alex begged.

Amy moved over to the left and gave me a look of concern. I instantly knew that Devon was going to open the door and grabbed Alex by the arm to move him behind myself and Amy.

If ever there was a time for emotions to be flowing, this was it, as every one of us was scared witless. And those emotions were very likely nourishing some very bad creepies just beyond the two inch metal door. Their pushing against the door had stopped. They knew what was coming as well.

Devon grasped the handle with her right hand and pushed down the latch with her thumb. Suddenly, there was no sound, nothing. No evil mumbling sounds were emanating from the stairwell and there was no pounding on the door. Devon swung the door open to reveal a mass of wretched looking soldiers, grotesque burn victims and random abominable people all awaiting their turn at our small group. Few had emotion on their faces and a few barely had faces.

At the front stood the large bony wraith appearing as a Confederate soldier who had just dispatched the young man seeking Devon's condition. His head was somewhat lowered and he was looking at Devon through the top portion of his eyes. His brow was set in a scowl and he looked very intense.

"Why did you kill that man?" Devon demanded in a firm believable voice. "You are here to protect."

There was a short pause as the wraith seemed to be looking directly through Devon and deeply into her soul.

"Shut up!" he screamed, showering Devon in vile spittle. "You don't know nothin'."

Devon raised her hand in an attempt to threaten the evil ghost but he was having nothing of the sort. With a horrific scream he launched himself at her grabbing her by the hair and lifting her by the crotch. He catapulted Devon into the air and through a nearby wall, just as Amy had done to the evil spirit in Chattanooga.

"Feel familiar?" he screamed at her as she disappeared into the darkness of the next room.

Suddenly, the room began to fill with wraiths of all different sizes and appearances and their target was Alex, Amy and me. The fight was on.

At first, the battle was defensive in nature for the three of us. Amy and I were forced to split our time between throwing punches and defending Alex. Occasionally, Alex would land a fist or connect with a kick, but mostly he was too weak, comparatively, to inflict much damage on our attackers. As we backed and fought our way away from the stairwell door, more evil ghouls were entering and lining up for their shot. I quickly realized that many of them were still the souls they were before they died.

Some would come charging at you in blind rage and with no self-control. They were easily dispatched either momentarily or, if I got a good enough hold on them, permanently. Others would lurk along the edge of the scrum, cowardly awaiting a sucker punch moment. This happened to Amy only once that I saw and a couple of times to me before we caught on to their M O. Amy being the older of the two of us obviously learned faster than me.

The third and last occurrence of this wraith sniping caused me to smile knowingly as I vowed mentally to not let it happen again. I grabbed the orphan boy who had done the sniping by the hair as he attempted to flee behind a larger wraith. He disappeared quickly as he likely was ready to go home and take his long overdue medicine from some long dead parents.

Amy was delivering some punishing blows that would completely disable some of our assailants. At that point she would provide cover as I would send them. She didn't seem to be using any of her angel abilities as none of them seemed to be disappearing. Perhaps these things were just too strong for her to simply evaporate. The system seemed to be working out pretty well, initially. The bigger more despicable wraiths would force the lesser ones into the fight in an attempt to test us. I guess it was their way of probing our defenses. It is also likely why Alex was able to have any success at all against some of them. Whatever their reasoning, it was quickly lowering their ranks. Why they didn't rush us all at once I will probably never know, but I was glad they didn't.

Within minutes, the wraiths had ceased entering the room and the three of us had established a semi perimeter with a wall behind us and the remaining ghouls in a semi-circle fronting us. There were twelve of them left, made up mostly of hardened soldiers, a few random men and one really pissed off looking woman whose hair was completely singed off her head. By this point I was feeling very confident. We had handled everything the scummy wraiths had thrown at us, literally. This became an obvious mistake;

after all, we were fighting angry spirits not some random frat boys on a drunken Friday night.

The arc of wraiths tightened a bit as they inched their way closer to us. There no conversation in the momentary pause of the conflict; so naturally, I felt the need to insert some cocky bravado.

"That's a good look for you," I said pointing to the hairless woman who had made her way closer to me.

In hindsight, this was a very bad move. In my overconfident state, I had forgotten a very important rule in dealing with an upset woman. Never, under any circumstances, make fun of a woman who is having a bad hair day, ever. Not to mention the fact that this woman had obviously been mad for a long time already and she was dead. You could literally see the anger well up in her cold lifeless eyes as she stepped toward me.

The blow she hit me with was open handed and came up from below my chin. The heel of her hand struck my jaw and I felt the back of my head strike the top of my shoulders. Rarely have I ever been hit this hard, let alone by a woman. Obviously, I had forgotten this was no ordinary woman anymore and there was a reason she was still here in front of us to fight.

Alex tried to catch me as I fell backwards from the blow. He missed. Amy never took her eyes off the group advancing on us. She knew what was coming. I did too, now. Shaking off the cobwebs, I staggered to my feet, another lesson learned in this classroom of evil soul fighting.

My confidence had been replaced with anger. This was a dangerous time as pure uncontrolled rage had been the one emotion Amy warned me about the most. The wraiths immediately picked up the sensation of my anger. They were also feeding off of Alex's growing fear. The boost these emotions were giving the wraiths emboldened them into advancing further.

Two of the soldiers came at Amy, grabbing her by each arm before she could react. A few feet away the large bony wraith lowered his shoulder and form tackled her, taking all three of them into the wall behind us. The woman who had taken me down with one punch now came at me with two other ghouls following closely behind her. I knew a kick was my best bet to get one of them before he could reach Alex and me so I launched a right leg into the air. It found its intended target and with the crack of several ribs, he crumpled to the ground. All I could accomplish after that successful first shot was flailing defensive blows as the burnt head woman and her counterpart were now upon me, scratching, grabbing and punching.

Amy regained her footing and was now locked in a desperate struggle to fend off her three aggressors. Each of them seemed delighted at the pain they could inflict on her and also surprised at the pain they felt when she landed a blow. For many of these souls, this was the first pain they had experienced in over one hundred and forty years and they would reel momentarily until they recovered and continued the fight.

So, there we were, in an all-out brawl with some of the most vile and angry souls ever to walk this portion of the Earth. There were no magic wands or swords, no weapons other than what God had given you when you entered this world; arms legs, hands, head and mind. The fighting was all hand to hand, physical, personal and violent. I had ripped off more than one ear or gouged an eye or two by this point and desperately attempted to prevent the same from happening to me. The group with the most physical strength and unwavering faith was going to win this bout.

All twelve of the wraiths remained when Alex was knocked out by a bony elbow from one of the other random wraiths. He had raised his hands, palms facing out, towards the wraith, just as he had done earlier in the day at my house. I instantly knew he was attempting, in vain, to use the powers he thought he possessed but did not. I now regretted allowing him to think he had those abilities. His face exhibited true surprise when this trick didn't work and the wraith used the opening to knock him out.

The moment he lost consciousness the wraiths were weaker, as his fear had been giving them sustained nourishment to this point. Before his body even completed its slide down the wall, the nearest wraith was in trouble physically. He had only one eye left and a broken jaw and the loss of Alex's fear seemed to complete the drain on him and he staggered sideways until his legs buckled under him and he collapsed to the floor.

In addition to the loss of Alex's emotions, I had gained control of my own anger and was now focused on channeling it from rage to desire, the desire to win the fight, that is. These two occurrences allowed the conflict to stabilize somewhat, however, Amy and I could not hold off the remainder of the wraiths much longer. Fatigue was now becoming an aspect of this battle as well and we were wrought with it.

Suddenly, there was movement in the shadows to my right. In a flash, a figure leapt out of the darkness and onto the back of the burnt woman who was attempting to separate my head from my body by way of a vicious head lock. She relinquished her grip on my skull and I slid out of her arm hold. I was shocked at what I saw. It was Devon, and she had both of her hands on either side of the woman's head, as if she were trying to crush it inwardly.

Within seconds, the woman melted into waxy black goo that quickly disappeared. I shot to my feet, not sure if I was her next target, not sure of anything at this point. Devon looked at me ashamedly and then turned to go after another wraith, which she quickly removed from the fray with a firm grasp of the back of their neck. She hurled the quickly disappearing spirit across the room and into the darkness.

The tide had now turned, Amy was continuing to battle the three strongest wraiths, including the large nasty one that had entered the room first, and Devon and I had begun to pick off the others. Two of the soldiers turned to run from the room. I was able to catch one but not the other. This particular coward thought it to be a good idea to attempt to bite me as I drew him closer. With a quick flip of my wrist, I grabbed his arm and twisted it behind his back. Feeling a bit angry about the attempted chomp, I decided to introduce the hand of the twisted arm to the top of his head. This shattered his shoulder and dropped him to his knees. The rest was easy, as he no longer had any fight left in him and with a shove downward on the top of his head he was gone.

As I turned, Devon was completing the dispatching of another evil soul with a strong grip on his throat. His arms were thrown open and back as if waiting for some sort of embrace. He vanished in this position. I was momentarily envious as I had not been able to accomplish a soul sending of such grandeur. Across the room I noticed there were only two wraiths left squaring off against Amy. Neither were the big bony one and I had a split second sensation of relief as I knew he was the strongest. If he was now gone, this would all be over soon. He wasn't.

From behind Devon, I witnessed him stand from a crouching position. She stood completely defenseless as she made eye contact with me from about twenty feet away. The look on my face must have tipped her off to the presence of something behind her and she quickly turned to face her attacker. It was already too late, he was upon her.

With incredible force, he punched her squarely in the center of her chest. The horrible sound of the bone crushing impact echoed through the room. Devon flew backwards, landing on her back and the base of her head, in no way able to brace herself for the impact with the floor. I lurched forward in an attempt to protect her. My first punch landed on the side of his face with a nice thud. The wraith shuddered for a brief second and then turned and landed a backhand forearm to my shoulder which sent me reeling across the room. The wraith now stood straddling Devon's motionless body. With an emotionless look across his face, he dropped both knees onto Devon's chest with the full force of his body.

Amy saw all of this occurring and forcefully shoved the wraith standing in front of her backwards. She was enraged by the actions of the wraith now pummeling Devon. In a quick motion with her right hand she grasped the air directly in front of her and the wraith that had only seconds before been fighting her was crushed to half his former width. With a swift motion she threw him aside, writhing in the pain of not being able to breath and not being able to die.

The large wraith was lifting his right hand to levy a blow to Devon's head when Amy reached him. She grabbed his arm in mid swing and yanked him from his perch on top of her. I quickly gathered myself and rushed to the side of Amy as she was beginning her anger driven assault on this soulless soul. Nothing the wraith did was working at this point. He could not free Amy's grip on his arm and he could not flee. With a flick of her wrist, Amy broke the wraith's arm at her point of grip. At the same time, she had grasped the other arm and subsequently broke that bone as well. She then moved on to his upper arms and then on to his legs, snapping each bone progressively with a rapid twist of her wrist. The wraith fell to the floor in a grotesque heap.

Amy then relinquished her grip on the wraith and I stepped over him, straddling him just as he had done to Devon. With my right hand, I gripped his temples and steadily increased the pressure, attempting to inflict as much pain as I could before he was gone. His skin felt cold and rough as I vehemently began the process of sending him on his way. I couldn't help but succumb to the urge to smack the back of his head on the wooden floor a couple of times for extra emphasis. The wraith never made a sound as he melted away into the floor. Once he was gone I spat on the floor where he had been laying. I was a bit upset with myself for not doing it sooner.

Across the room Alex was beginning to stir and groan softly as he slowly awakened. Devon lay motionless where she had originally fallen, showing no outward signs of life. Her eyes were open in a lifeless stare and her mouth was agape. There was a small trickle of blood from the left corner of her mouth and her forehead was bruised from the earlier impact with the wall.

"Devon," I called out to her in a raised voice intended to bring her out of her unconscious state.

With my right hand I attempted to attain a pulse from her neck. There was none. I grasped her right wrist in a search for any signs that her heart was still pumping blood. There was no pulse at her wrist either. I placed my ear over her mouth to listen for breathing and when I heard none, I began a frantic attempt to give chest compressions.

Amy was kneeling beside me. Her face showed little expression as she lowered her head.

"You can stop now, Zach," a familiar voice called out. It was Devon's.

"I was dead the moment he struck my heart," Devon's voice continued, trailing off at the end of her statement.

I looked around struggling to find the source of Devon's voice. Amy too began to search the room as she slowly stood. Within a few seconds, there was a figure forming right in front of us. At first it was only the outline of a female, but it quickly became obvious it was Devon. There in front of Amy and I stood the soul of the woman that had been duped into causing much of the carnage of the past few months. She appeared calm and confident and had a knowing look on her face.

"Devon?" I said shocked to see her ghost standing there.

"I'm sorry about your father," Devon said with sincerity. "I never intended for any of that to happen. I was told that you were stealing souls, for evil, maybe even the Devil. I never imagined for a second it was actually me. You know, I came here tonight thinking I could stop all of this. I guess I got what I deserved."

"It's okay," I said in response. "You were under the influence of a very persuasive entity."

"Yeah, but my gut told me otherwise and I should have listened," Devon said. "You know that little voice inside your head? Yeah, it was right. Throughout my life, I always liked to think that was God talking to me."

"It was, basically," Amy added.

I shot her a "stop it" look and she responded with a one shoulder shrug and a "well it was" return glance.

"I know it was," Devon added with a smile. "Well, I need to go."

"Do you want me to...," I began but was halted by Devon's raised hand.

"No," she responded quickly. "No, I have some work to do here still; maybe some other time, though. I'll see you again."

"Are you sure?" I pleaded. "Don't you want to go to a better place than this?"

"Oh I do, just not yet," she answered. And then she was gone.

We gathered Alex and guided him to the stairwell. He was still very groggy and I felt there was no need to give him any of the details he had missed in his unconsciousness. Making our way down the stairs, we were greeted by the occasional body of one of the invitees. Many of them had obviously been attempting to reach the top floor for some sort of shelter against the rage of the wraiths which had run amuck throughout the building.

A few of their souls had not yet left and were still very close to their bodies. When we would meet them, I would send them on to a better place. Most of the dead understood what had happened and what I was doing. Some however, didn't want to go anywhere just yet, just like Devon. This didn't surprise me as these were people who had devoted at least some of their lives to ghosts and now they were one of these entities they so desperately searched for. They obviously didn't want to let go of the opportunity. I couldn't force them so we went on without helping them. Once again, I was amazed at how free choice really did seem to shape so much of our lives, both before and after death. I also knew I would likely encounter them one day in the future.

The walk back to the Tahoe didn't seem to take as long as I remembered a few hours earlier. We hurried down the dark streets, not wanting anyone to notice Alex and his hampered appearance. Once we reached the vehicle, I fought the urge to fall asleep right there in the driver's seat. The one thing keeping me awake was the faint but ever present feeling of not being alone. There were still spirits everywhere around us.

By the time we returned to the house, we were beyond exhausted. The sun would rise in a few hours, revealing November in all of its late fall glory. Alex made his way to a warm and soft spot on the carpet in the bedroom and fell fast asleep. I collapsed onto the couch and stared up at the ceiling. Amy stood next to me for a moment. When she realized how quickly slumber was coming to me, she smiled and nodded.

"You did good little brother," she said in a reassuring tone.

"Thanks," I responded. "I am gonna take a quick power nap."

"Go ahead, I'll be here when you wake up," she answered.

Immediately, the dreams of exhaustion shot through my subconscious. Quick flashes of images or replays of recent occurrences jolted my body into twitches and starts. Amy softly placed her hand on my forehead and I fell deeply into the most comfortable sleep imaginable. She had been here before, many times over many years. She always enjoyed doing this. I slept. We weren't done. She took a seat on the arm of the couch and there she stayed, watching over me as I slept.

Printed in the United States
By Bookmasters